Welcome to the world of St Piran's Hospital

Next to the rugged shores of Penhally Bay lies the picturesque Cornish town of St Piran, where you'll find a bustling hospital famed for the dedication, talent and passion of its staff—on and off the wards!

Under the warmth of the Cornish sun Italian doctors, heart surgeons, and playboy princes discover that romance blossoms in the most unlikely of places…

You'll also meet the devilishly handsome Dr Josh O'Hara and the beautiful, fragile Megan Phillips…and discover the secret that tore these star-crossed lovers apart.

Turn the page to step into St Piran's— where every drama has a dreamy doctor… and a happy ending.

Dear Reader

Many years ago I was lucky enough to visit Cornwall, and I absolutely loved it. The contrast between the sandy coves and the coast, where the surf crashes onto wild rocks. The stretches of rugged farmland and the villages with gorgeous old cottages. The Cornish cream teas…mmm.

I've always wanted to go back, and the invitation to be part of the *St Piran's Hospital* series was irresistible. Not only could I revisit—at least in my imagination—the physical setting, I could get to know the people I'd already enjoyed meeting in Penhally a whole lot better.

Best of all, I got a really tortured hero. I've never had one quite as dark as my Luke, but it was amazingly easy to fall in love with him. Just like Anna does.

I hope you do, too.

Happy reading!

Love

Alison

ST PIRAN'S:
THE BROODING
HEART SURGEON

BY
ALISON ROBERTS

First published in Great Britain 2011
by Mills & Boon,
an imprint of Harlequin (UK) Limited,
Large Print edition 2011
Eton House, 18-24 Paradise Road,
Richmond, Surrey TW9 1SR

GIFT

© Harlequin Books S.A. 2011

Special thanks and acknowledgement are given
to Alison Roberts for her contribution to the
St Piran's Hospital series

ISBN: 978 0 263 21762 9

Alison Roberts lives in Christchurch, New Zealand. She began her working career as a primary school teacher, but now juggles available working hours between writing and active duty as an ambulance officer. Throwing in a large dose of parenting, housework, gardening and pet-minding keeps life busy, and teenage daughter Becky is responsible for an increasing number of days spent on equestrian pursuits. Finding time for everything can be a challenge, but the rewards make the effort more than worthwhile.

Recent titles by the same author:

THE MARRY-ME WISH*
WISHING FOR A MIRACLE*
NURSE, NANNY…BRIDE!
HOT-SHOT SURGEON, CINDERELLA BRIDE
THE ITALIAN SURGEON'S CHRISTMAS
  MIRACLE

*Part of the *Baby Gift* collection

ST PIRAN'S HOSPITAL
Where every drama has a dreamy doctor…
and a happy ending.

Nick Tremayne and Kate Althorp
finally got their happy-ever-after in:
ST PIRAN'S: THE WEDDING OF THE YEAR
by Caroline Anderson

Dr Izzy Bailey was swept off her feet
by sexy Spaniard Diego Ramirez
ST PIRAN'S: RESCUING PREGNANT CINDERELLA
by Carol Marinelli

The arrival of Italian neurosurgeon Giovanni Corezzi
is guaranteed to make your heart beat faster
ST PIRAN'S: ITALIAN SURGEON, FORBIDDEN BRIDE
by Margaret McDonagh

Last month, daredevil doc William MacNeil
unexpectedly discovered that he's a father
ST PIRAN'S: DAREDEVIL, DOCTOR…AND DAD!
by Anne Fraser

This month the new heart surgeon
has everyone's pulses racing
ST PIRAN'S: THE BROODING HEART SURGEON
by Alison Roberts

Fireman Tom Nicholson steals Flora Loveday's heart in:
ST PIRAN'S: THE FIREMAN AND NURSE LOVEDAY
by Kate Hardy

Then newborn twins could just bring a marriage miracle
for Brianna and Connor Taylor
ST PIRAN'S: TINY MIRACLE TWINS
by Maggie Kingsley

And finally playboy Prince Alessandro Cavalieri
comes to St Piran
ST PIRAN'S: PRINCE ON THE CHILDREN'S WARD
by Sarah Morgan

CHAPTER ONE

IF LOOKS could kill, Luke Davenport would be a dead man.

Dr Anna Bartlett had finally deigned to join him in Theatre for her assigned job of assisting him in a potentially complicated procedure, and she was clearly less than impressed that he had decided to go ahead without her.

Sure, he'd received a message while reviewing his patient's notes that she was caught up in the emergency department of St Piran's hospital with a chest trauma case requiring a thoracotomy and would therefore be late, but what had she expected? That he would delay the case until she arrived? This patient had already had to wait longer than he should have for his surgery. In any case, if the patient in Emergency survived the aggressive procedure to try and stabilise him, Dr Bartlett would be the only person available to take them to another theatre and that left Luke in precisely the same place—having to find someone else to assist him in surgery. Thankfully, this wasn't that difficult given the talented staff this hospital could boast, and paediatric cardiac surgeon James Alexander had been available and only too willing to assist the returning head of department.

James had joined the staff in the eighteen months Luke had been away. He was not only settled in the area but married to Charlotte, a senior registrar in the cardiology department. Just one of a countless number of changes. So many it was hard for Luke to imagine he'd once been a part of all this. It was frightening how one's world could change in a heartbeat.

Like Luke's had done when the news of his younger brother's death had rocked the seemingly solid foundations of his life and prompted the radical decision to join a military medical unit. Nothing would ever be the same and yet here he was, trying to pick up the pieces of his old life.

If it felt wrong to him, it was no wonder he was an unwelcome disturbance in Anna Bartlett's world. She'd had enough time to become part of this medical community. To stake a claim and make this department her own. Maybe that was the real reason for the resentment he could detect. That he was in charge again.

It would be a bit of a blow to anyone's ego, wouldn't it, being bumped from a position as top dog? Everybody had known that his replacement was temporary but nobody had expected him to return so abruptly. Maybe Anna had secretly thought he might never return from Iraq. To add insult to injury, it wasn't the first time Luke had taken the position from her. He'd been the winner three years ago when he'd been chosen over her for the prestigious role of head of St Piran's specialist heart surgery unit.

Yes. That could well explain the death glare he'd caught from over the top of the mask as

Anna had finally entered the theatre. She stood outside the cluster of staff around the operating table now, gowned and masked, her gloved hands held carefully away from her body. Taller than average, he noted in that split second of noticing her arrival, and her eyes were green. Very cool right now because she was displeased and that made them seem hard—like uncut emeralds. Unusual enough to make a lasting impression. As did her body language. The way she was standing so absolutely still. It advertised the kind of attention to detail, like not contaminating anything, that came from being not only well trained but highly disciplined.

He'd heard that about her from James as they'd scrubbed in together. That his missing assistant was skilled and meticulous. Uncompromising. Single because she chose to be. Or maybe no man could compete with a job that someone lived and breathed to the exclusion of anything else.

'She's good,' James had added. 'Very good.

You'll be pleased she's taken on the job of Assistant Head of Surgery. With the reputation she's built here, she could have gone anywhere she chose.'

James obviously respected Dr Bartlett but he'd also said he didn't really know her. Not on a personal level. The way his sentence had trailed off in a puzzled tone had suggested that maybe she didn't have a personal level.

It was James who acknowledged her presence now, however.

'Anna! That was quick.' He gave his colleague a closer glance and frowned. 'No go, huh?'

'No.' The word was crisp. The attempt to save someone in the emergency department had failed. That was that. An unsuccessful case. Time to move on to the next. 'Want me to take over?'

'If that's all right with Luke. I am rather late to start my ward round now and I've got my own theatre slot this afternoon.' James sealed another small blood vessel with the diathermy rod and then looked up at the surgeon across the table. 'Luke? Have you met Anna already?'

'No.' His response was as curt as Anna's verdict on her emergency case had been.

He carried on with the long, vertical incision he was making in his patient's chest, not looking up until James moved in to control the bleeding.

She was standing closer to the table now. A mask covered the lower half of her face and a disposable hat hid her hair and ears. All he could see were those green eyes and for a split second the accusation in them hit home.

Yesterday he had been supposed to meet the woman who'd looked after his job for eighteen months, but there'd been that hassle at his house with a burst pipe and there had been no water supply. There'd been a problem getting power reconnected as well, after such a long period of being empty, so he'd had no way of recharging the battery for his mobile phone when it had died. The hassles had underscored the fact that he wasn't exactly thrilled to be back here anyway and…and she hadn't waited for him, had she? He'd been less than an hour late but she had gone home and hadn't left any message other than the theatre list for this morning.

And now she was glaring at him as if accepting her belated assistance for this surgery was only the first challenge he had coming his way. Well, she could take her attitude and deal with it on her own time.

'If you plan to assist,' he said curtly, 'now's the time to start. I don't like my surgeries being disrupted and I'd prefer to start the way I mean to go on.'

A tense silence fell around them as James stepped back and Anna smoothly took his place. The familiar ache in Luke's leg kicked up a notch but that only served to increase his focus. He turned his head to the scrub nurse hovering over the trolley beside him.

'Sternal saw, thanks.'

The nurse jumped at his tone and handed him

the requested item with commendable speed. Then the whine of the saw cut into the silence he could still feel around him. Luke concentrated on splitting the bone beneath his hands. For a short time at least, he had no need—or inclination—to look at the woman now opposite him.

So this was Luke Davenport.

The war hero she'd been hearing so much about in the last few days. Too much. As if it hadn't been bad enough to have her position as head of department cut short, no one hesitated in rubbing salt in the wound by telling her how marvellous Luke was. What a great surgeon. And soldier. How he'd single-handedly saved everybody he had been with when they had come under attack, dragging them from a burning vehicle despite his own badly broken leg and then providing emergency care that had kept them alive until help arrived.

She could believe it. One glance from a pair

of the most piercing blue eyes Anna had ever seen and she knew she was meeting someone just as ambitious and determined as she was herself. Two horizontal frown lines at the top of his nose, between dark eyebrows, added to the intensity of the glance and made her catch her breath. To have him treating her like a junior fresh out of medical school might be unacceptable but it wasn't totally surprising. This man had seen and dealt with things she couldn't begin to imagine experiencing.

'An honourable discharge from the army,' someone had said. 'He's up for a medal.'

St Piran's was so lucky he had come back. The hospital, the patients, the whole damn community was feeling lucky. Anna had had to hide disappointment strong enough to morph very easily into burning resentment. Had to try and smile and pretend she felt lucky that she was being given the opportunity to be the hero's assistant from now on.

No wonder the guy was so full of himself he

hadn't even bothered to come and introduce himself yesterday. She'd given him the courtesy of sending an apology for being late for this theatre case and look at his response! He didn't like his surgeries being disrupted. The voice had been deep and the words clipped. This was a man who was not only used to giving orders, he expected them to be obeyed.

Anna's spirits—already well dampened by the unsuccessful struggle to save a life in Emergency—slipped a little further. The only way through this, as she'd discovered with any previous difficult episode in life, was to focus on her work to the exclusion of anything else.

It wasn't hard. 'Good grief,' she couldn't help but comment when the rib spreaders were locked into position and the target of this surgery was exposed. 'Look at that.'

The sac of membrane enclosing the heart had calcified and become a thick, white casing—a kind of scar from the inflammation a virus had caused and so solid it was preventing the heart from beating effectively. Luke was about to perform a pericardectomy and peel this hard layer away from the heart tissue. A tricky, fiddly procedure that Anna had studied but never performed herself.

She would have been happy enough to do the surgery if a better option hadn't been available, but she would definitely have preferred to have the patient on bypass and a still heart to work with. Luke was sparing this man the additional risk of being on a heart-lung machine. He was going to do the procedure with the heart moving beneath his scalpel.

'Your investigations showed the extent of the calcification.' Luke sounded mildly surprised by her exclamation of astonishment. 'Right-sided filling was poor and the stroke volume was abysmal. It's a wonder he's been able to function at all.'

'The first sign that it was anything serious only came when he collapsed at work three weeks ago.'

Anna watched as Luke used a scalpel to cut through the hard, white tissue, his hand large enough to make the small instrument almost invisible. She could see how much pressure he was needing to apply but how careful and controlled that pressure was. He needed to open the scarred tissue but not penetrate the heart beneath.

His response of a grunt to her statement could have actually been satisfaction at the gleam of healthy, pink tissue revealed, but Anna caught something that seemed more like a reprimand that it had taken that long to diagnose the condition correctly and arrange livesaving treatment.

The criticism was unfair. This patient, Colin Herbert, had avoided even going to his GP for years, putting his shortness of breath down to being unfit and his tiredness to the broken nights of helping to parent two young children. Even initial investigations hadn't pointed to a cardiac cause for these symptoms in the thirty-seven-year-old. It had taken a CT scan and then cardiac catheterisation to reveal the rare condition, and that had left Anna having to decide whether to attempt an unfamiliar surgery herself or refer Colin to someone more experienced.

The news of Luke Davenport's return had made it worthwhile delaying the surgery for just a little longer. If Colin could stay in St Piran's, close to his family and friends, it would probably speed his recovery. It would certainly make this period far less stressful for his wife and children.

Luke had now begun peeling the pericardium away from the heart muscle. The anaesthetist, amongst others, was peering into the wound with fascination.

'Looks like plastic,' one of them commented.

Another grunt came from the surgeon and then silence fell in the theatre again. His requests for instruments or responses to updates on monitoring were curt. He barely acknowledged Anna's assistance. Surgery with this man was never going to be a relaxed affair, then. Not that he shouldn't be concentrating fiercely on the task at hand, but that had never stopped Anna from involving her colleagues. Testing their knowledge and sharing her own. Discussing problems and allowing contributions to any trouble-shooting needed. The way mentors had done with her in the past.

Being Mr Davenport's assistant might be like treading water as far as her career was concerned. Demoted to second best but only allowed to learn anything new by observation. Anna could feel the frustration creeping in already. She might well have to bite the bullet and start fighting for the chance to prove herself elsewhere. Having to apply for sought-after positions where most of the applicants, as well as those making the final choice, were male. Skilled, powerful, alpha men like the one working opposite her right now. Men who needed a lot of convincing that a woman was capable of being their equal.

But even as Anna felt the tightening knot of a

tension she'd been aware of for her entire career in medicine, something else was pushing into her awareness. The skill Luke was demonstrating here told her that, merely through observation, she could learn from him. His timing was exquisite as he allowed the heart to beat and squeeze out blood, then advancing his scalpel to free the casing a little further in each fraction of time when the heart was filling again and, therefore, still enough to be safe.

The equipment and the technician needed to put the patient on bypass were standing by. Peeling the pericardium from the back of the heart would be the most difficult part of this procedure and Luke was keeping the option of using cardiac bypass available.

He would prefer not to, however, and so far things were going smoothly. The staff were more than competent and he had no complaints about Dr Bartlett's assistance. She was good. Somehow she had instantly tuned in with how he worked, and it was like having an extra pair of his own hands in action. Smaller hands, of course. More nimble ones. It was quite possible that Anna would be better suited to continue this when he got to the tight patches around the back.

The thought was embryonic. Barely registered, in fact, because Luke was so focused on what he was doing. Anna had the edge of the hardened pericardium caught in a pair of forceps, holding it up and helping to peel it away as he cut carefully beneath it.

He was using the scalpel with absolute precision. Tiny cuts as close to the hard casing as possible. There was less than a millimetre of space to work in. Luke was vaguely aware that the atmosphere around him was tense and that he could change it by relaxing a little and talking more, but he had no desire to do that.

He was being watched in this, his first surgery on returning to his role as head of department for cardiac surgery. Being watched and judged.

They were wondering if his experience in the army had changed him—as a surgeon or as a person.

Of course it had. He had honed skills and one of them was the ability to focus no matter what kind of distractions were around. What anyone else, including Anna—no, especially Anna— might be thinking of him was irrelevant. What mattered here was a good outcome for his patient. His focus was on that scalpel. Right on its tip, which was the only part of the blade he was using.

The blood seemed to come from nowhere. There'd been small bleeders up to now that Anna had dealt with but this was a sudden gush that drowned his scalpel, washed over the fingertips of his gloves and began to form a pool. The beat of the heart made it appear briefly and then the blood washed over it again, totally obscuring his vision.

Red.

So red.

And warm. He could feel it on his fingers. Sticky life blood, ebbing rapidly from where it was supposed to be.

Someone was dying.

He could hear their screams. He could hear the sound of gunfire, too, and smell something burning.

He had to do something.

But he couldn't move.

Anna saw the moment the small artery got nicked by the tip of the scalpel. It needed more than diathermy. Clamping and tying it off shouldn't present more than a momentary delay. She picked up a clamp, ready to hand it to Luke, already eyeing up the suture material he would need.

But he didn't request the clamp. The hand that was holding the scalpel was as still as stone. Frozen.

And then the surgeon looked up, straight at her, and Anna's own heart missed a beat. He was looking at her but he was seeing something very different. Something that had absolutely nothing to do with this room or this patient or the surgery he was in the middle of performing.

He was seeing something…terrifying?

Her heart missed only a single beat. With the next one she was moving smoothly. Using the clamp in her hand and then a suture. To those around them, it would look as though Luke had silently requested her control of the nuisance bleeding. Given his virtually silent technique up until now, it wouldn't have surprised anyone. But Anna had been the only one to see the look in his eyes. Had felt the way he had frozen, and it had quite possibly been the most disturbing moment she had ever encountered in Theatre.

It took only moments to deal with the artery and a nurse used suction to clear the operating field again. Anna heard Luke's indrawn breath and looked up to see the way he blinked with such deliberation it gave the impression of a switch being flicked off. And then normal service was resumed. The surgery carried on as though nothing awkward had happened.

But something had changed. Maybe it was an acknowledgment of the way Anna had rescued the situation. Or maybe it was the beginning of the kind of bond that could weld a tight team together.

'If I tilt the heart,' Luke said quietly a short time later, 'you're in a much better position to deal with that patch at the back. Are you happy with what you've seen of the technique?'

'Yes.' The increase in her own heart rate wasn't trepidation. It was far more like excitement. The challenge of trying something new. The idea that she might be on a new journey to learn skills that nobody else could teach so well. There was something like relief mixed in there as well because her future here at St Piran's looked a little less bleak. There was even a letting go of a little of that resentment towards the man who had reclaimed his job. The job she had desperately wanted to keep.

Thank goodness her hand was steady as she took hold of the scalpel. Even better was Luke's quiet praise as he watched what she was doing.

'That's excellent. Keep going. The more of this we can remove, the better the outlook for this patient will be.'

By the time the surgery was complete, the outlook was good and Luke finally stood back from the table and stripped off his gloves, thanking everyone for their contribution to the successful procedure. As he turned to leave, he tugged at his mask, breaking the strings that held it in place, and for the first time Anna saw more than those intensely blue eyes.

She saw a rugged, unsmiling face, with deep furrows from his nose to the corners of a mouth wide enough to balance the size of his nose. He wasn't what you'd call classically good-looking but it was hard to look away. The raw, unpolished masculinity was compelling. Those frown lines were still there at the top of his nose so maybe they were a permanent feature. When

Luke started tugging off his bloodstained gown as he neared the swing doors of the theatre, Anna saw the lean muscles of deeply tanned arms. She could have sworn that those doors opened of their own accord, which was impossible but there was something about the commanding height and the way this man moved that made the notion perfectly feasible.

Luke Davenport was a soldier as much as—or possibly more than—he was a surgeon.

Every female in the room was watching as he made his exit, no doubt equally impressed, but Anna knew she would be the only one who found the image conflicting. Downright confusing, really.

Yes, Luke had lived up to his reputation as a gifted surgeon and he was apparently prepared to let her close enough to absorb valuable new skills but…what the heck had happened back when that bleeding had occurred?

Was Luke even aware of the way he had zoned out like that? He certainly hadn't acknowledged her contribution to the situation. He'd been injured during his time on the front line. An injury that was serious enough to prevent his return to his army position. Maybe he'd received wounds to more than his leg? A head injury perhaps that had left him with a form of epilepsy? Absence seizures where the sufferer was unaware of their surroundings and could freeze for up to a minute or so would explain it, but if that was the case, there was no way he should be still holding a scalpel.

That explanation didn't seem plausible, however. A seizure would have someone looking blank and Luke hadn't looked blank at all. He'd looked... *Haunted* was the word that sprang to mind. As though he'd been sucked into a flashback that he hadn't been able to escape from. This seemed far more likely but no less excusable.

What if he'd been close to the pulmonary artery? Or, worse, the aorta? Even a few seconds of delayed response in trying to control the kind of bleeding those vessels were capable of producing could have been disastrous. What really bothered Anna was knowing that she was probably the only person who had noticed the incident, which meant that saying anything might be seen as a form of professional sour grapes. Revenge, even, for the reprimand she'd received because of her late arrival for the case. Everyone knew that she'd missed out on the job as departmental head when she'd first applied. Now they'd be watching to see how she was handling her new role. To make an accusation that could have major repercussions on Luke's career within the first few hours of them working together was unthinkable.

There was only one person who might accept and understand her concerns. The same person who could provide an explanation that could possibly negate the need to take it any further. If nothing else, Luke deserved the courtesy of direct communication but it was also a conversation that needed to happen in private.

Right now her focus had to remain with their patient as he went into Recovery and was then settled into the intensive care unit for monitoring and post-surgical care. She had surgery she was due to perform with a registrar to remove sternal wires from a patient who'd had heart surgery a long time ago but was continuing to suffer pain that was probably a reaction to the foreign material in her body. The procedure wouldn't take too long and she'd planned to use her lunch break after that to talk to Luke and suggest a detailed ward round to bring him up to speed with all the cardiac inpatients.

Maybe she'd better use that time for something rather more personal. To make a judgment call on the integrity of the man she had to be able to trust if she was going to work with him at all. For some reason, the prospect of getting that close to Luke Davenport was more intimidating than anything Anna could remember facing.

She needed to think of it as nothing more than

a new professional challenge. Backing away or trying to make it easier was not an acceptable option. She'd take it face on. Anna gave a decisive nod as she followed Colin's bed out of Theatre. She actually found herself almost smiling, having made the decision to confront Luke. If the situation had been reversed she had no doubts at all that Luke would be addressing the issue. He would probably have done so on the spot, with no thought of sparing her the humiliation of an audience.

Maybe this was a subtle opportunity to demonstrate not only her ability to do the job he had reclaimed but that her way of doing it might be better.

The prospect of the private interview with Mr Davenport was no longer simply intimidating.

It was…exhilarating.

CHAPTER TWO

THE need to escape was overwhelming.

And impossible.

Having ripped off the theatre scrubs, Luke had gone straight to the showers in the changing room but he couldn't wash away the aftermath of those few seconds in the middle of Colin Herbert's surgery. Turning the water to lukewarm hadn't brought its recent comfort of familiarity. Even the icy cold blast he finished with couldn't shock it out of his head the way it could chase nightmares away.

His clothes felt wrong, too. His trousers and an open-necked shirt felt too smooth against skin used to the thick fabric of camouflage overalls. At least he didn't have to knot a tie around his neck, like tying a bow on a pretty parcel. How ridiculous would that seem when he would far rather be fastening the Velcro straps of a Kevlar bulletproof vest over his shoulders. Feeling the weight of the armour plating and the bulkiness of pockets stuffed with whatever he might need at a moment's notice.

He felt too light as he strode out of the theatre suite without a backward glance. Almost as though he was floating.

Lost.

The corridors were full of people going about their business, but it was all so slow. There was no sense of urgency as beds and wheelchairs were propelled to new destinations or staff moved from one task to another. They had time to stop and chat to each other. He saw people smiling and even heard laughter at one point. Someone said hello to him and Luke managed to smile back, but the facial contortion felt grim.

He didn't belong here any more. This was a joke that wasn't the least bit funny. Like the whole of civilian life. It was a game. A pretence. Meaningless.

Going outside was better. A brisk walk around the sprawling, modern structure that was busy St Piran's hospital. A helicopter was coming in to land, no doubt bringing a trauma patient to the emergency department. Luke's eyes narrowed as he watched it intently and soaked in the sound of its rotors. If anything was likely to give him a flashback, surely that was?

It wasn't going to happen. He knew that because he was aware of the potential and he was focused. In control. The way he should have been for every second of that surgery. He kept watching anyway. Testing himself, until the helicopter took off again and disappeared into the distance.

A tempting distance. He could start walking again and just keep going. Stride down the cobbled streets of this picturesque market town until he got to the harbour. Or, better yet, a stretch of beach where he could push himself with the added difficulty of walking in sand. Or hurl himself into the surf with its magic, albeit temporary, ability to numb his body and brain and wash everything away. An effect a thousand times better than a cold shower.

But this was early December. It was freezing and his wetsuit was hanging to dry on his back porch after his early swim that morning. His leg hurt, too, thanks to standing so still for so long in Theatre. And he was here because he had a job to do. A job he had been lucky to be able to come back to. An anchor. Something to build on and the only thing he had, really. Given time, this might start making sense again, giving him the bonus of feeling like he was doing something worthwhile even, though after this morning that goal seemed further away than ever.

At least the patient who had been unfortunate enough to be his first case back here was doing well.

It was nearly an hour later that Luke arrived in the intensive care unit and Colin was awake, though very drowsy. A nurse was by his side and she smiled warmly at the surgeon.

'I've been hearing all about the surgery,' she said to him. 'I wish I could have seen it. I hear you did an amazing job.'

Luke made a noncommittal sound without looking away from the monitor screen giving detailed recordings of what was happening inside Colin's heart thanks to the catheter that had been positioned at the very end of the surgery.

Surgery that could have been a total disaster. An amazing job? He didn't think so.

The nurse was still hovering. He heard the intake of her breath. She was about to say something else. Possibly another admiring comment. Luke shifted his gaze to give her what he hoped would be a quelling glance. Sure enough, her mouth snapped shut, a flush of colour stained her cheeks and she turned to fiddle with an IV port on her patient's arm.

Colin's eyes flickered open. He saw the surgeon standing beside his bed and smiled weakly.

'I'm still here,' he said, his voice slightly raspy. 'Thanks, Doc.'

Luke returned the smile. 'You're doing fine. We'll keep an eye on you in here for a bit and there's a few tests we need to run later today, but we'll get you onto the ward as soon as possible. Do you have anything you want to ask me about?'

Colin's head moved in a slow shake. 'I think my wife's asked everything already. Dr Bartlett seems to know what she's talking about. I'm still a bit groggy to take it in but I'm alive and that's what matters.' He smiled again, his relief obvious.

'I'll be back later. I can talk to you and your wife then.'

'Dr Bartlett said how well things had gone. What a great job you did.'

'Oh?' That surprised him. Or did Anna not worry about embellishing the truth when it came to reassuring her post-operative patients?

'The wife's just gone to find my mum downstairs and look after the kids so Mum can come in for a visit. Hey, did I say thanks?'

'You did.'

Luke knew he sounded brusque. He didn't need the nurse to give a look vaguely reminiscent of the glare he'd seen more than once in Theatre from Anna. Did she know? Had word spread that his new colleague had had to leap in and prevent the error he'd made during surgery becoming a potential catastrophe?

'Where is Dr Bartlett?' he asked the nurse as he signed off a new addition to the drug chart and prepared to leave the intensive care unit. 'I need to have a word with her.'

'Back in Theatre, I expect.'

Of course she was. He'd seen the case listed on the whiteboard in the theatre suite. A sternal wire removal. In the same theatre Colin had been in. With the same theatre staff, presumably. Would Anna be checking whether anyone else had noticed the incident and could back up her report on the concerns she now had about the abilities of the returning head of department?

She hadn't said anything at the time. Hadn't even sent a significant glance in his direction, but that said something in itself, didn't it? She hadn't bothered to hide what she thought of him returning to take her job in those early glares. It suggested that she was weighing the implications. Making sure she used the ammunition he had handed her to best effect by choosing the best time and place.

Dammit! How the hell had it happened? He was well used to the nightmares, but to have a flashback like that happen during the day? In the middle of surgery? It was appalling. He wasn't quite sure of how long he had lost his focus but he had no doubts about what could have happened if there hadn't been someone as quick as Anna on the other side of that table.

It wouldn't happen again. He'd lost focus because that had been his first slot back in a civilian theatre. His concentration had been too much on a procedure that couldn't have been more different to the kind of work in an Iraqi field hospital or, more particularly, as a member of the medical emergency response team on a mission on the front line. It had been slow and fiddly compared to the aggressive, lifesaving measures of treating major trauma under circumstances as tough as they got. It had been a mental ambush, triggered by the unexpected amount of blood he'd seen, or the way it had pooled, maybe.

Whatever. It wouldn't happen again because he'd be ready for it and wasn't going to allow a loss of control. Luke was perfectly confident of his ability to do just that.

But would Anna believe it?

A pair of green eyes came to mind. Framed by dark lashes that were unadorned by any mascara. Angry eyes. Accusing and assessing at the same time. What would they be like, softened by trust?

Even more compelling, no doubt, but Luke

had to wonder if he would ever witness such a change.

Winning Anna's trust was not even the priority it probably should be because this underlying tension…this waiting for something potentially unpleasant to happen, was oddly welcome. It made him feel a little more alive than he had ever felt since he'd been shipped home.

He was there, in the hospital canteen. Sitting alone near a window.

Brooding was the word that sprang to Anna's mind. Hunched over a plate of food he appeared to be toying with rather than eating. The big room was well populated and noisy. Was that why the table with its single occupant seemed to stand out like a beacon? Or was her glance drawn there like a magnet because so many other people were eyeing the newcomer and probably talking about him?

She could understand not wanting to be in there and either listening to or being the object of the kind of speculation and gossip rife in any group of people as large as the St Piran's staff was, but why on earth hadn't he done what she almost always did—buy a sandwich and some fruit to take back to the privacy of an office?

Was he hoping for company? There must be so many people there who knew him but there was a hierarchy involved and maybe there weren't any of his peers around. Anna found herself hoping that by the time she got to the end of this long queue someone would have joined Luke. That way, she wouldn't need to feel guilty about not doing so.

Not that she didn't want the chance to talk to him, but this was hardly the place to have the kind of conversation she had in mind, and the idea of making small talk with this man was not appealing. It would be dishonest, in a way, when they both knew what needed to be discussed—the kind of game-playing Anna had never had the slightest inclination to indulge in. Besides, Luke was making himself look so very unapproachable. Self-contained and cool. If he knew and agreed with all the praise going on behind his back, his self-image would have to be more than a little inflated. Maybe his own company was enough?

Like Anna, Luke had changed out of his scrubs and was dressed neatly. Professionally. Anna slid her tray along the metal bars in front of the food cabinets and found herself running her hand down the side of her close-fitting skirt to make sure it wasn't creased. And then touching her hair to ensure that no tendrils had escaped the sleek knot at the back of her neck. She could do professional, too. Better than anybody, which was no surprise given the amount of practice she'd had.

'Anna… Hi!'

A new burst of hungry staff members was milling behind her, settling into the queue. The greeting had come from Charlotte Alexander, one of St Piran's cardiology staff members, who was behind a couple of nurses who'd stopped to stare into a chilled cabinet containing rolls of sushi.

If Anna made personal friendships among her colleagues, which she didn't, Charlotte would have been at the top of her list. While their relationship was friendly, it was still as professional as Anna could keep it. Even now, when the loose top Charlotte was wearing reminded her that she'd noticed the obvious increase in weight a week or two ago and it had occurred to her that Charlotte could well be pregnant, she wasn't about to ask such a personal question.

Girl stuff, like heart-to-hearts or sharing secrets and especially wedding or baby talk, was never going to happen. They were in the same category as frilly clothes or loose hair or make-up. Badges of femininity. Barriers to acceptance as an equal in a male-dominated profession. How did women like Charlotte manage it? Looking and dressing in a way that accentuated their best features but still having the respect of both colleagues and patients?

It made Anna feel like she had some kind of split personality, but it was so engrained now it was getting hard to know whether it was the Anna at home or the Dr Anna Bartlett at work that was the real her. The only thing she could be sure of was that never the twain could meet.

But sometimes…like right now…it struck Anna that her work persona was simply armour. Concealing anything feminine and vulnerable. Giving her focus and strength. Her gaze strayed of its own accord back to the solitary figure of Luke Davenport. What was it about him that made her even more aware that she didn't look as feminine or, God help her, attractive as she could? Just as well her work persona was so firmly engrained. If armour was what it was, she might need its protection more than ever.

Charlotte had been held up too long. She moved around the nurses who couldn't decide between the teriyaki chicken or smoked salmon.

'Hi.' She smiled at Anna. 'How's it going?'

'Very good. Theatre's over for today and both

patients are doing well. I just took the sternal wires out of your Violet Perry. I'm sure the irritation will be gone and she'll be pain-free in no time.'

'That's great.' Charlotte was peering into the sandwich cabinet. 'Hmm. Chicken and Camembert sounds nice. Or turkey and cranberry. No…we'll be sick of that soon. Have you seen how many Christmas decorations are up already?'

'Mmm. Way too soon, in my opinion.' Anna found the seasonal celebrations at work disquieting. Too much of a bridge to personal lives.

'Ham salad,' Charlotte decided, reaching for one of the triangular plastic boxes. 'Oh…weren't you in Theatre with Davenport this morning? Doing Colin Herbert's pericardectomy?'

'Yes.' Again, Anna's gaze strayed towards Luke.

'How did it go?'

For a split second Anna considered confiding in Charlotte. Telling her all about how Luke had frozen and she'd had to take over the surgery. If she did, she'd be taking a step she could never undo. Charlotte would tell her husband, James, and the snowball effect might sweep them all into places they would rather not go. This man was going to be her professional partner from now on. They would be working closely together. Closer than she was with Charlotte or James or any of the other cardiology or cardiac surgery staff. She and Luke would share duties in Theatre, on ward rounds, during outpatient clinics.

As though he sensed her stare, Luke raised his head to look up. Straight at Anna. Just for a heartbeat she held his gaze and tried to analyse what she could feel in that connection.

Maybe he wasn't bad tempered and brooding, she decided as she looked swiftly away. Strangely, for that moment in time, it had looked more like something deeper. Possibly even unhappiness? What reason could he have?

He had been forced to leave the army early

due to his injury, hadn't he? Perhaps Luke didn't want to be here just as much as Anna didn't want him to be.

She looked away but not before she felt an odd squeeze beneath her ribs. She knew what it was like to feel unhappy.

Lonely.

Did she really have to kick someone who might already be down? Maybe she was over-reacting. She had stepped in so fast, after all. If he'd been about to move at the same time it wouldn't have been such a big deal at all. Not that she'd had the impression he would have moved that fast, but it wouldn't hurt to think about things a little longer.

'It was amazing,' she heard herself telling Charlotte, absently picking up a pack of chicken sandwiches. 'I've never seen a technique quite that precise. I got to do a patch behind the left ventricle and it wasn't easy.'

'Wish I could have seen it,' Charlotte sighed.

'Did you know he'd ordered the observation deck closed?'

Her disappointment was clear. It was an opportunity to express caution about the man's personality or even say something negative. Curiously, Anna felt the need to defend Luke.

'I guess you wouldn't want too many people watching when you're doing your first case after a long time away.'

'I guess. How's Colin doing now?'

'Really good. We might be able to move him to the ward later today. Tomorrow, anyway, if he stays this stable. We should be well past the danger period for complications from acute dilation of cardiac chambers but his heart's still got to get used to dealing with much more of a blood flow.'

'I'll get up to see him this afternoon. Here's hoping the surgery report won't be far away. I'll be very interested to read it.'

So would Anna, but her agreement was silent. If she'd voiced it, her tone might have suggested that there would be more to read about than Charlotte might expect. They were getting near the cashiers' part of the counter now and she turned her attention to the baskets of fruit. An apple, she decided. The nice-looking green one on the top of the second basket.

The crash that came from somewhere in the kitchens behind the food counters was astonishingly loud. Metallic. Jarring enough for every head in the cafeteria to swivel sharply in that direction and for conversation to cease abruptly.

And in that second or two of startled silence a scream rang out. And then a cry for help.

Jaws dropped as staff members looked at each other as though trying to confirm the reality of what was happening. Anna heard Charlotte's gasp behind her but she was watching something else. Weirdly, her instinct had been to look away from the source of the sound so she had seen the first movement in the crowd. A reaction time so fast it was hard to process.

Luke Davenport was on his feet. His chair tipped backwards and he pushed at the table in front of him rather than stepping around it. The table also tipped, the tray sliding off to send china and cutlery crashing to the floor but Luke didn't even spare it a glance. He was heading straight for the kitchen.

Access was blocked by the tall, glass-fronted cabinets apart from the space where Anna was, beside the tills and the fruit baskets. There was a flap in the counter beside the last till where kitchen staff could go in and out with the trolleys of used dishes but Luke didn't bother to stop and lift it. Or maybe he didn't see it. He swept the baskets clear to send apples and oranges bouncing around the feet of those still standing motionless and then he vaulted the space, making the action seem effortless.

Kitchen staff were backing away hurriedly, but not quickly enough for Luke.

'Move!' he barked. 'Clear the way. What's happened?'

'Over here,' someone shouted. 'Oh, my God…
I think he's dead.'

Luke took several steps forward. Between
the tills, Anna could see the blue uniforms of
kitchen staff moving. Clearing a space near the
stoves in front of which a large man in a white
jacket lay very still.

Luke took in the scene. He turned his head
with a single, rapid motion.

'Anna!' he shouted. 'Get in here. I need you.'

Someone had raised the flap now but, if they
hadn't, it occurred to Anna that she might have
tried to leap over it, too. Luke needed her?

The man was obviously one of the chefs. His
white hat had come off when he'd collapsed
and was lying amongst the pots and pans of an
overturned rack.

Luke kicked one of them aside as Anna raced
into the kitchen. 'Get rid of those,' he ordered.
'Someone help me turn him. Did anyone see
what happened?'

'He just fell,' a frightened woman offered.

'One minute he was cleaning down the cooker and then he toppled sideways.'

'What's his name?'

'Roger.'

The man had been rolled onto his back now. Luke gripped his shoulder and shook it firmly, hunched down so that he could lean close and shout.

'Roger? Can you hear me? Open your eyes!'

He barely waited for the response that didn't come. His hands on Roger's chin and forehead, he tilted the head back to open his airway.

'Does anyone know him?' he demanded. 'Medical history?'

'He takes pills,' someone said. 'For his blood pressure, I think.'

'No, it's his heart,' another voice added.

The few seconds that Luke had kept his fingertips on the side of Roger's neck and his cheek close to his face had been enough to let him know that there was no pulse or respiration to be felt or seen. Anna crouched on the other side of the collapsed man as Luke raised his fist and brought it down squarely in the centre of the man's chest. A precordial thump that was unlikely to be successful but was worth a try.

Ready to start CPR, Anna was thinking fast, compiling a mental list of what they would need. Luke was way ahead of her.

'Get a crash trolley in here. Find a cardiac arrest button. Send for someone in ED or wherever's closest. Anna, start compressions.' He looked up at the silent, horrified onlookers. 'Move!'

They backed away. Anna heard someone yelling into the canteen for the cardiac arrest button to be pushed. If there wasn't one in there, it wouldn't be too far away. She positioned her hands, locked her elbows and started pushing on Roger's chest. He was a big man and it was hard work to compress the sternum enough to be effective.

Ten…twenty…thirty compressions. At least someone would arrive with a bag-mask unit very soon so she didn't have to worry about the implications of unprotected mouth-to-mouth respirations on a stranger.

The faint possibility of contracting something like hepatitis didn't seem to occur to Luke. Or it didn't bother him.

'Hold it,' he ordered Anna, pinching Roger's nose and tilting his head back as he spoke. Then he sealed the man's mouth with his own. One slow breath…and then another.

Anna started compressions again, the image of Luke's lips pressed to someone's face emblazoned in her mind. The kiss of life… She'd seen it before, though it was a rarity in a medical setting. Was that why it was so disturbing this time? Shocking, in fact. She had to concentrate on her silent counting until it was time to warn Luke.

'Twenty-seven, twenty-eight, twenty-nine, thirty…'

By the time they had completed another set

of compressions and breaths, there were new voices nearby and the rattle of a trolley.

'Crash team,' someone announced. 'We'll take over now.'

'I've got it, thanks,' Luke growled.

'But it's what we—'

'We just need the gear,' the surgeon interrupted. 'And some assistance.'

Anna could feel the resentment at not being allowed to do what they thought they had been summoned for, but a life pack was lifted from the trolley and put on the floor along with an IV roll, a bag mask and a portable oxygen tank.

She carried on with the chest compressions, pausing only to let Luke rip the chef's jacket and the singlet underneath open to expose the chest and stick the pads in place. On direction, one of the doctors in the crash team secured his airway and attached oxygen to the bag mask, holding it in place until Anna paused again.

Could she ask to hand over compressions to someone else? This was enough of a physical effort to make her aware of perspiration dampening her shirt. No, she wouldn't ask. She was with Luke on this.

He had been the one to respond and identify the crisis, which made this man his patient until he chose to hand him over. And he'd asked for Anna's help. Roger was their patient and they could do this as well, probably better, than the junior doctors assigned to crash-team duties for the day.

'Stop compressions.' Luke was watching the screen of the life pack, waiting for a readable trace to appear. 'V fib,' he announced moments later. 'Charging to three hundred joules. Everyone stand clear.'

The junior doctors inched back, exchanging glances.

'Who is this guy?' Anna heard one of them ask another.

'Luke Davenport,' came the response. 'You know, the surgeon who's just got back from Iraq?'

'Oh...'

In the short space of time it had taken for three stacked shocks to be delivered, the atmosphere in this inner circle around the victim changed. The crash team, who had been busy resenting not being allowed to showcase their skills in managing an arrest, suddenly couldn't do enough to help their leader.

'Do you want an intubation kit, Mr Davenport?'

'Shall I draw up some adrenaline? Atropine?'

'Here's a sixteen-gauge cannula. And a flush.'

'Dr Bartlett? Do you need a break?'

Anna sat back on her heels, nodding. There was plenty of scientific evidence that compressions became less effective after two minutes unless someone else took a turn. She didn't move far away, however. She watched, totally amazed by the speed at which Luke worked. And she noticed things she hadn't noticed before.

Like the streaks of grey in his short brown hair. They had to be premature because she knew he was only a few years older than her and couldn't have hit forty quite yet. He had such neat fingernails too and his hands looked so different without gloves. Far more masculine, which made their speed and cleverness more impressive as he gained intravenous access and secured the line.

His brain was working just as fast. He seemed to be able to think of everything at once and keep tabs on what everybody was doing, but most of all, Anna was caught by the way he'd taken a trolley of equipment and a group of young medics who hadn't been thrilled not to be allowed to take over and forged them into a team that was now working under difficult conditions as well as they could have in a re-suscitation bay in Emergency.

It was a team that had achieved success even before Luke had made a move to secure Roger's airway with an endotracheal tube. When the static cleared from the next, single shock delivered, the flat line suddenly gave a blip. And then another…

'Sinus rhythm,' one of the crash team said triumphantly. 'Yes.'

'Have we got a stretcher?' Luke still hadn't relaxed. 'Let's get this man into the ED. Or CCU.'

Charlotte had edged her way to the back of the kitchen. 'Great job, Mr Davenport. Would you like to hand over now?'

'Call me Luke,' he said, still watching the monitor. The rhythm was picking up steadily and Roger was taking his own breaths now. The chef's eyes flickered and he groaned loudly.

And, finally, Anna saw the grim lines of Luke's face soften a little. He leaned down and gripped Roger's shoulder again with his hand— the way he had when he'd first begun this resuscitation effort. He didn't shake it this time. This was a reassuring touch.

'Just relax,' he told Roger. 'We're looking after you. Everything's all right.'

He looked up at Charlotte and gave a nod to indicate transfer of responsibility. Charlotte moved closer to talk to him, but as she moved, Luke shifted his gaze to Anna.

And something inside her tightened and then melted.

From the moment this incident had started—from when she'd heard the scream and seen Luke's instantaneous response, she'd been aware of his total command of the situation. Of his faultless performance and ability to absorb additional resources and personnel and then… right at the end…an indication that he really cared about this patient.

An impressive mix. If his glance had been in any way smug, it could have driven Anna into a defensive corner she might never have emerged from, but there was no hint of smugness. No self-satisfaction even. The fraction of time he held her gaze sent a message that was more like, We did it. This time, at least.

The triumph that was there was on the patient's behalf. Behind that was the acknowledgment of defeat in other cases and the sadness that they couldn't always win. Shining over both impressions was a kind of promise. A determination to always fight the odds and do the best possible job.

It sucked her right in.

She could work with this man. Could respect him. Like him.

More than that, in fact, judging by the odd ripple of sensation that caressed her spine and sent tingles through the rest of her body.

Dear Lord, she was attracted to him? No wonder she'd been so aware of her own appearance when she'd been standing in line with Charlotte. It explained a lot but it was a reaction that had to be crushed instantly. Allowing something that personal to threaten a professional relationship would be the ultimate play on femininity.

The reason women couldn't be seen as equals in this arena was largely because of the perception that they allowed emotion to cloud their judgment. Or, worse, they put a priority on relationships and undermined their careers by taking time off to have babies.

Not Anna Bartlett. It wasn't on any agenda she'd ever had.

Luke's return and—worse—his attractiveness were roadblocks. Ones she could detour around, which would see her working somewhere else, or deal with if the pull to stay put was strong enough. Either way, getting even remotely close to Luke Davenport would be a mistake.

It was Anna who broke the eye contact.

And turned away.

CHAPTER THREE

THE crisis over, Luke found he couldn't drag his eyes away from Anna.

Not that he hadn't spotted her the moment she'd walked into the canteen. He'd taken a good look then because he hadn't been sure it was her. Something about the height and body shape of the woman had seemed familiar but he'd only seen her eyes before this so it could have been anybody.

Just an attractive female member of staff. A senior member, obviously, because of the way she held herself. The way she moved with the confidence of someone who knew she was very good at what she did. And maybe he recognised something in the way this woman was dressed. Power dressing, really, with that pencil skirt and neat shirt. She probably had a matching jacket that would make the outfit the female equiva-lent of a man's suit. And what was that horrible thing she'd done to her hair? It was all scraped back into a round thing that made her look like a cartoon version of a librarian or frumpy sec-retary. All she needed was some thick-rimmed spectacles to complete the picture.

When her head had turned to scan the room, he hadn't needed to be close enough to see the colour of her eyes to recognise that this was, indeed, Anna Bartlett. While she wasn't radi-ating resentment right now, there was an air of containment about her that suggested she didn't change her mind easily. A reserve that could well morph into an arctic-type chill when she saw him. A woman that knew her own mind and woe betide anyone that got in her way. Like him.

Luke almost sighed as he dropped his gaze back to a meal he wasn't particularly interested in. He wasn't enjoying this lunchtime experi-ence much at all, in fact. He knew that many of the people around had to be talking about him. Gossiping. The happy chatter and laughter going on around him, even the smell of abundant, hot food all seemed irrelevant. Superficial.

The crash and then the scream had been real, though. He'd reacted on autopilot. He wasn't sure what had made him demand Anna as an assistant. Possibly because she had been the only staff member nearby that he could call by name. Or maybe it was the memory of how well they had worked together in Theatre only a short time ago.

It had been a good choice. The crisis had been dealt with and a life had been saved and it had only been then, when it was virtually done and dusted and he was handing his patient into the care of a new team, that Luke had allowed anything else to enter his head. It was then that he'd had his first close-up look at Dr Bartlett and he'd had the curious impression that he'd been looking at something he wasn't supposed to be seeing.

No wonder! The cool professional he'd seen queuing for her lunch was absent. This woman, standing in the canteen kitchen with a creased skirt and a shirt that had come untucked on one side, was…wrong, somehow. Even more disconcerting was that a thick lock of dark blonde hair had escaped the bun thing and lay against a long, pale neck.

Her cheeks were flushed. From the exertion and stress of doing CPR or was she embarrassed at being dishevelled? Even her eyes looked different. Enlarged pupils made them seem softer. Warmer.

Good grief…she was rather lovely.

Any impression of warmth vanished, however, as Luke stared at her, unable to drag his gaze away.

And then she dismissed him! Simply turned on her heel and walked away.

How rude. No genuine warmth there, then. Anna Bartlett was clearly a career woman through and through, and she probably saw him as nothing less than an obstacle in her scramble to the top of that ladder. Any hope that she might discuss this morning's incident with him before reporting it to a higher authority faded and disappeared.

Charlotte, the cardiologist, was saying something to him, he realised. Something about whether he'd like to come with them to the emergency department to see what the investigations Roger needed would reveal.

'Yes,' he said. 'Please.'

'You'll remember Ben Carter?'

'Of course.'

'And have you met Josh O'Hara? No, you wouldn't have. He joined the A and E staff while you were away.'

Luke kept up with the pace set by the people pushing the stretcher, heading away from the canteen and any areas that his assistant was likely to be heading for.

He'd see Anna again soon enough. Doing a ward round later today or perhaps in the departmental meeting scheduled for early tomorrow morning. Given how he felt about her in the wake of that dismissal, it might even be too soon.

The aura of the war hero already surrounding the return of Luke Davenport to St Piran's had evolved into something far more tangible by the time Anna was halfway through her ward round later that afternoon.

He had become a living legend.

Thanks to the crowd in the canteen at the time, accounts of the incident would have spread like wildfire and reached every corner of this institution in no time flat. Spilling into ears eager for the smallest details.

The junior nursing staff on the cardiology ward were discussing it when Anna paused outside the central station to collect some patient notes she needed.

'It was like something in the movies,' someone was saying in awed tones. 'He just pushed everything off the counter and jumped over it.'

'I heard he did mouth-to-mouth without even using a face shield.'

'Yeah…'

'Is the guy still alive?'

'Apparently he's in the cath lab right now. He'll probably get admitted in here or CCU when they're finished.'

'Do you think Mr Davenport will come down with him?'

'Ooh…I hope so.'

The giggling from the young nurses was irritating. Anna decided it was because her own participation in the incident had been totally eclipsed by the actions of St Piran's new superhero. Except that she couldn't convince herself to be that petty. The irritation was really there because part of her was as star-struck as everyone else seemed to be. The man was intriguing. Compelling. Apparently trustworthy. And that was disturbing because Anna felt that she knew something about him that no one else knew. Or would believe.

If she wanted to discuss her concerns with someone, the obvious choice would be Albert White, the CEO of St Piran's. He would listen to any concerns she might have about Luke's abilities. He might even believe her and, if he did, he might set some kind of probationary programme in place. Things like that did not remain confidential. Eventually, it would leak. Given his performance in the canteen and new status amongst the staff, nobody else would believe Anna.

She might find herself more alone than she'd ever been in her struggle to break through the glass ceiling of her gender. It could affect how well she was able to do her own job. She stood to lose the trust and possibly even the co-operation of the people she worked with and teamwork was vital in this line of work.

Tread carefully, she reminded herself, even when her demotion from being team leader had been rubbed in when a flurry of activity had heralded the new arrival in the coronary care unit adjacent to the ward and more than the necessary staff numbers flocked to greet both the patient and the new head of department.

Roger the chef was made comfortable and wired up so that every beat of his heart could be monitored, the trace and its extra information like blood pressure and the level of oxygen in his blood appearing on one of the screens flanking the central nurses' station. It was there that Luke caught up with Anna.

'He needs urgent revascularisation,' he informed her. 'I'm hoping you can fit him in on your list for tomorrow.'

Anna closed her eyes for a split second as she groaned inwardly. She opened them to find herself under intense scrutiny.

'Is that a problem?' Luke asked. 'You don't have any elective patients on the list?'

'I do, but I've just been talking to a Mrs Melton and reassuring her. She's stable but has severe triple vessel disease. This is her third admission for surgery because she's been bumped off the list for urgent cases on the last two occasions.'

'Has she had a major infarct? An arrest?'

'No.'

'Come and look at Roger's films and then we can discuss it. Have you got viewing facilities in your office?'

She did, but Anna was aware of a strong reluctance to take Luke there. She had chosen not to take over his office in his absence and her space was relatively small. It was also the most personal space she had here at work.

She was already a little too aware of this man. His size and reputation and…and whatever it was that was exerting a tugging sensation on something emotional. Not to mention the danger that frisson of potential attraction had represented. She didn't want him invading a personal space. Not yet. Not until she felt a lot more confident in her interactions with him and that wasn't going to be until she'd resolved the dilemma she was in.

'The seminar room's closer. Where we hold the departmental meetings.'

'Of course. Have you got the time now?'

'Yes. I've finished the ward round.'

The round Luke had been supposed to join her for, but if he noticed any reprimand in her dry tone he gave no indication of it. He led the way down the corridor, his pace fast enough to keep Anna a half step behind. The hint of asymmetry in the way he moved had become a noticeable limp by the time they reached the lifts but Luke didn't pause. He pushed open the fire-stop doors and headed up the stairs.

Commenting on something as personal, not to mention physical, as the aftermath of his injury seemed inappropriate. In the same ball park as asking Charlotte if she was pregnant, and this wasn't remotely like the far more social setting of the hospital canteen with its 'time out' from work atmosphere. This was work and Luke's focus was entirely professional. He had no difficulty using the computerised system to bring the images from the catheter laboratory onto the large screen in the meeting room.

'As you can see, there's a seventy to eighty per cent stenosis on the left anterior descending and diffuse disease over a significant segment of the vessel. And that's not all. There's a critical stenosis in the circumflex. Here…see?'

'Yes.' Anna watched and listened. It was quite obvious that Roger was in more urgent need of surgery than her Mrs Melton. As the head of department, Luke would have been within his rights to simply order her to juggle lists but instead he was taking the time to put all the information in front of her, presumably with the intention of giving her the opportunity to make the call.

Exactly the way they should be interacting as colleagues. There was every reason to take a moment to admire the way he was dealing with the situation but there really shouldn't have been any space in Anna's head to be so aware of the way Luke moved his hands as he spoke. Of how elegant those movements were for those large hands with their clever, tapered fingers.

It was quite reasonable to appreciate the way he spoke so clearly too and the transparent speed with which his mind worked, but that didn't excuse the enjoyment Anna found she was getting from the timbre of that deep voice. She brushed off the visceral reactions. So he was intelligent and articulate. She should have expected nothing else in someone who had beaten her in a job application.

But perhaps that underlying awareness of him as a person and not simply a surgeon made her more aware of his physical issues. When they had finished coming to a mutually agreeable compromise on theatre lists, which would see Mrs Melton staying on as an inpatient until her surgery could be scheduled, Luke stood up. His face was grim and he blinked with slow de-liberation, as though he was in pain but determined to ignore it. Or switch it off. The action took Anna straight back to their time in Theatre that morning and she knew she couldn't avoid broaching the subject.

'How's your leg?' she found herself asking. 'I understand you suffered a fairly serious injury?'

'I survived.' Luke's tone told her it wasn't a welcome subject for discussion. 'It's improving all the time.' His stare was expressionless. 'Why do you ask?'

Anna had to fight back the urge to apologise for asking a personal question. His eyes were so blue. So intense. No way could she simply dismiss that sharp squeezing sensation occurring deep in her belly. It might have been a very long time since she'd experienced a shaft of desire but it was all too easy to recognise. She looked away.

'I've taken on a position as your assistant. If you have problems that I could help with, please don't hesitate to tell me.'

Luke made an incredulous sound, as though

Anna would be incapable of giving him any assistance. That she had no idea what she was talking about. The sound rankled. She looked up to meet his gaze again.

'If, for example, you find it hard to stay on your feet for a long theatre session.'

A corner of his mouth lifted. Just a fraction. A sardonic twist but enough of a curl for Anna to realise she had yet to see Luke smile. He certainly wasn't about to now. His expression was anything but friendly or relaxed. Her heart skipped a beat and then sped up but it was too late to swallow any words that had been spoken and try to get back onto safe ground.

She had seen his pain when Luke knew how good he was at hiding it, and it seemed like he was exposing a physical flaw. Almost as bad as that loss of focus in Theatre that morning had been. Anna had been the only person to pick up on that, as well.

He'd barely met the woman and yet it felt like

she was inside a very personal space. As for offering to help with his problems. Ha! She didn't know anything.

No one here did.

And yet the idea was appealing. To have someone in his corner who was prepared to listen even if they couldn't begin to understand.

To have someone to hold at night…

Whoa! Where the hell had that come from?

Luke could manage being alone. He had to. Just as well he'd learned to bury the kind of emotional involvement that could make reality too hard to deal with. He might be back in a very different reality now but the ability to remain detached at some level was just as important. More important, maybe, given that he felt the despair of a meaningless existence pressing in on him from all sides.

He was looking into a future that had only one bright spot. His work. And Anna was trying to undermine it. Something like fear made him straighten and defend himself by attacking.

'Are you suggesting I'm physically incapable of doing my job?' He had her pinned with his gaze. 'Hoping that it might prove too much and I'll quietly go away and let you take over again?'

He saw her eyes widen and felt a flash of remorse at being so harsh. He also heard the swift intake of her breath but he didn't give her time to speak. He couldn't afford to back down. Admitting defeat wasn't something Luke Davenport did willingly.

'This is my home,' he continued. 'Where I live and where I work. Where my future is. I'm back and I have no desire to go anywhere else.'

Which one of them was he trying to convince here?

'I wasn't suggesting anything.' Anna's tone was clipped and very cool. 'Maybe I was hoping there might be a satisfactory explanation for what happened in Theatre this morning. For your slow response to a significant bleed.'

A moment's silence hung heavily between

them. Not that Luke had any intention of deny-ing the accusation or trying to excuse himself.

'I lost focus,' he admitted simply. 'It won't happen again.'

He saw the way her features softened at his honesty. She wanted to believe him. But he could also see confusion in the depths of those astonishing green eyes. What had he been thinking, attacking her for asking what had been a perfectly reasonable question? No wonder she felt torn.

'Are you intending to report the incident?'

She held his gaze. She had courage, this woman.

'Would you?'

'Yes,' Luke responded without hesitation. 'Sloppy performance is never acceptable.'

Anna tilted her head in agreement but said nothing. They left the meeting room in silence. There seemed to be nothing more to be said.

So that was that. The subject was out in the open and he'd all but told her he expected it to be reported. All he had to do now was wait until someone, presumably Albert White or one of the other hospital administrators, came to have a little chat with him.

It didn't happen the next day.

If anything, Luke got the impression that Anna hadn't said anything at all about him that wasn't complimentary, judging by comments made in the departmental meeting the next morning.

More than one member of the cardiology and cardiothoracic surgical staff said admiring things about Colin Herbert's surgery. The congratulatory buzz when Roger's case came up during the discussion on revised theatre lists was actually embarrassing.

Luke cut it short. 'I had some very able assistance from Dr Bartlett,' he told the group briskly. 'And she's the one with the real work to do with his CABG today.'

That coronary artery bypass grafting was well

under way by the time Luke left his administrative tasks and headed for the theatre suite. He didn't don a gown or mask and enter the theatre. Instead, he slipped quietly into the observation deck and sat, probably unnoticed, in the far corner. You could see what was going on and hear what was being said and, if you wanted, you could focus on one person and make judgments about their ability. Their personality even. That was why he had requested that the space be closed during his surgery yesterday. An unusual case would have attracted as many people as could have squeezed in here and, on some level, he would have been aware of it.

Anna wasn't aware of him. He could watch every movement and hear every comment. He could feel the time and care she took with every meticulous stitch as she took the veins harvested from Roger's legs and used them to make new conduits to take blood to where it was needed in the heart muscle. Her voice was as calm as her movements. She was polite in her requests and prepared to discuss anything with the anaesthetist or bypass machine technicians. She spoke frequently to her registrar as well, asking questions and explaining her own decisions. A natural teacher, then.

With a voice that he couldn't imagine getting tired of listening to. Not when it was coupled with a brain that was clearly as focused but as flexible as her hands were. An impressive mix.

He stayed where he was only until the blood flow in the new coronary arteries was deemed acceptable and Roger was successfully taken off bypass. He would see Anna again today and maybe she would let him know who she had decided to speak to. He couldn't pre-empt her by speaking to someone himself because that would make it a bigger issue than it actually was. It wasn't going to happen again because he was in control now. Of every waking moment, at least.

But nothing more was said about it despite

their paths crossing frequently when they shared a busy outpatient clinic and more than once during ward rounds and departmental meetings. By Friday, both Colin and Roger were on the ward and recuperating well and finally, late that afternoon, Luke got a call to the office of St Piran's chief executive officer.

'Luke.' Albert White shook one hand and gripped Luke's other shoulder at the same time. 'I'm so sorry this has taken so long. It's been a hectic week that included a day or two in London. Welcome back. It's good to see you.'

'It's good to see you too.' And it was, except that he could feel the distance between them. He'd been on another planet since he had last worked here. But Albert was a familiar face. Part of the anchor that Luke hoped to use to stabilise his life.

'How's the family?'

'All well when I last heard any news.'

'I was astonished to hear that your parents had taken off to New Zealand, of all places. I hear they're living on a military base in North Island?'

'They are indeed. Dad's taken an administrative position. He calls it a semi-retirement but I can't see him ever not being full-time army.'

'No. And your older brother?'

'Currently in Australia. Helping train their SAS.'

Albert shook his head. 'Army family through and through. At least we've got one of the Davenport boys back again.'

'Yes.' The word was clipped. Luke didn't want to discuss the 'Davenport boy' who would never make it back.

There was a moment's silence, which seemed appropriate, and when Albert spoke again his tone was more serious, acknowledging so many things that were not going to be said.

'How's the leg?'

'Oh, you know. Still attached. Still works. I'm not complaining.'

Albert chuckled. 'Works pretty well from

what I've been hearing. What's with the commando techniques in the canteen? Leaping tall buildings on the agenda, too?'

Luke summoned a smile. 'I don't think so.'

'Well done, anyway. I hear the chap's doing really well.'

'He is. Dr Bartlett did a quadruple bypass on him. She's an excellent surgeon.'

'She is indeed.' The glance Luke received held a hint of relief. Any awkward subjects were being left well behind. 'So things are working out, then? You two going to be able to work as a team?'

Luke couldn't detect even a hint that the CEO might be fishing for any confessions regarding a bumpy start. Maybe he should say something about it himself but if Anna had chosen not to, perhaps he should respect her decision. Albert didn't seem to notice that his silence was covering a moment of confusion.

'Not that I expected any problems, but it was

good to hear Anna singing your praises the other day. A pericardectomy, I hear?'

'Um…yes. First case. What did she say?'

'That you did the entire procedure off bypass. That she was delighted to have the opportunity to learn something new.'

About the procedure? Or about him?

This meeting was nothing more than touching base. A welcome home.

'Come and have dinner some time soon. Joan would love to catch up.'

'Sure. Maybe when I've had time to find my feet properly.' Luke hoped his vague acceptance would not seem rude but he wasn't ready to get drawn into a segment of the St Piran's community that knew his family so well. He wasn't here because of the family connection. He was here because he'd had nowhere else to go.

Besides, he was getting into a routine now. An icy swim in the ocean at daybreak to chase away the night's demons. As many hours as possible focused entirely on his job and then exercise and work-related reading until he was hopefully exhausted enough to sleep for more than a few hours. He didn't want to tamper with what seemed to be working. Or remind himself of the past, which would only emphasise too clearly how different life was now. Control was paramount.

Control could be undermined by confusion, however. Anna had had a whole week to decide how to present her concerns about his skills but she hadn't done so.

Why not?

Not that Luke wasn't grateful but he was definitely puzzled. She'd agreed that the matter should be reported. That sloppy performance wasn't acceptable. And yet she had apparently accepted his.

Why?

He would have spoken to her about it before leaving work that day but it was late and she had already gone. It wasn't hard to use his influence to find her contact details but Luke discovered that she was living well along the windy coast road that led to Penhally.

A phone call to thank her for making his first week back smoother than it might have otherwise been seemed too impersonal. What he said might even be taken the wrong way—tacit approval for not reporting the incident perhaps. Taking a fifteen- or twenty-minute drive to what was quite possibly only a small collection of dwellings and knocking on her door after dark was a long way too far towards the other end of the spectrum, however. Far too personal. Why was he even considering it?

It didn't seem nearly as inappropriate on Saturday morning. Especially as the world in general seemed a brighter place. Days and days of grey skies and intermittent rain had been blown inland by a stiff sea breeze and the sun was making a determined effort to raise the temperature by at least a degree or two. The surf had been high enough that morning to make his swim an adrenaline rush, and his leg hadn't collapsed under him when he'd attempted a slow jog on the softer sand.

Yes. For the first time since arriving back, Luke felt that things were a little less bleak. Some time out on a day like this to drive up to Penhally and revisit old haunts was an attractive idea. He might have intended to wait until Monday to give Anna the excellent article on restrictive cardiomyopathy he'd come across in one of the journals he'd been reading until the early hours of that morning but if it was in the car, he'd have the perfect excuse to drop in at her house on his way past if he chose to.

He did choose to.

Maybe because the signpost to the lane she lived on was so easy to spot. Or perhaps because the house he found at her address was so unlike what he might have expected. Not even a house. More like a cottage with its latticed windows and some kind of evergreen creeper scrambling along the faded shingles of its roof.

The small garden was overgrown and…it had a picket fence, for heaven's sake!

If someone had asked him where he thought Dr Bartlett would be living, he would have imagined a modern apartment. Streamlined and minimalist. Devoid of personality—hers or its own. This cottage probably had tourists stopping to take its picture and a name somewhere under the tangled, prickly branches obscuring half the fence. Bay View Cottage perhaps, given the glorious sweep of Penhally Bay on display. It was only a short walk down the hill to get to a beach and, given the rocky coves he had noticed just before turning off the main road, the coastline was due to provide one of those gems that surfers searched for.

Sure enough, when he left the car and went a little further uphill towards the front door of the cottage, he could see a stretch of white sand beyond the boulders. This cottage might be run-down but it was sitting on valuable land. Any closer to Penhally or St Piran and it would be worth an absolute fortune. Was that why Anna had chosen it? As an investment?

That made far more sense than a desire to inhabit what had to feel like an alien space. Having come to terms with the apparent contradiction, Luke was now hesitant in knocking on her door. Had he passed a letterbox? He could leave the article in there and then explain it on Monday.

He might have done exactly that if it hadn't been for the sudden loud noise from inside the cottage. A crashing sound not dissimilar to the one he'd heard in the canteen earlier in the week.

No scream followed the sound but he could hear the dismay in Anna's voice.

'Oh…no!'

CHAPTER FOUR

'ANNA?' Luke didn't bother knocking. He tried the doorhandle and found it turned, so he shoved the door open. 'Are you all right?'

There was no response. Cautiously, Luke advanced along the narrow hallway. He could hear Anna's voice again. It was much quieter now. Soft and soothing.

'It's all right,' she was saying. 'Poor baby, you gave yourself a big fright that time, didn't you?'

Maybe he was in the wrong house.

'Anna?'

'Who's there?'

'Me,' Luke said as he stepped into a doorway on his right.

'Luke? Good grief! What on earth are you doing here?'

She sounded surprised. No, more like appalled. Luke opened his mouth but no words emerged. This was Anna?

She was sprawled on the floor, her arms around a large dog that was virtually in her lap and making enthusiastic attempts to lick her face. There were newspapers spread around them both, a collection of paintpots and an aluminium stepladder lying on its side.

'I was just on my way to Penhally. I heard the crash.'

'From the road?'

'No…I…er…had an article I wanted to give you.' It was weirdly hard to string a coherent sentence together so Luke gave up. He stared at Anna instead, trying to take in the faded, ripped denim jeans she was wearing. The paint-stained jumper. The soft waves of her loose hair that reached her shoulders. Those amazing green eyes that were staring at him in utter bewilderment right now.

Luke dropped his gaze. The dog was staring

at him too. Warily. Pressing itself further into Anna's arms and visibly shaking.

'What's wrong with the dog?'

'He's scared.'

'Of what?'

'You.'

She should probably be scared herself, Anna thought. A large man she hardly knew had just come into her house uninvited. Into her bedroom. Well, it would be her bedroom again when she'd finished renovating it. Right now it was just a mess.

Like her head.

Luke was wearing some jeans that were probably as old as her own. He had a black woollen jumper on with the sleeves pushed up to reveal bare forearms. His hair looked windswept and there was a tension about him that suggested he could leap into action at any moment. To save a life or rescue a damsel in distress.

He'd thought she was in distress.

He'd come into her house to rescue her.

And here he was, looking rugged and grim and...and...gorgeous.

Thank goodness she had her arms full of warm, shivery puppy. She hugged him more closely.

'He's a rescue puppy,' she told Luke. 'I've only had him a couple of weeks. My neighbours, Doug and June Gallagher, own a farm and they found him in the creek. In a sack. They would have kept him but they've already got a lot of dogs and he was terrified of Doug. June reckons he's been badly treated by a man.'

'So you took him? You're going to keep him?'

He sounded as though she'd just informed him that she intended to fly to the moon. Anna almost laughed but she felt absurdly close to tears. This wasn't supposed to happen and the earth had just tilted beneath her feet.

Dr Bartlett didn't do feminine or personal. She didn't do attraction to her colleagues.

Mr Davenport wasn't supposed to meet Anna.

And there were no rules about Anna feeling attracted to a man. There hadn't needed to be for too long to remember.

This was threatening to do her head in completely so she dragged her gaze away from the towering figure by the doorway and buried her face in the expanse of woolly hair in her arms.

'You're all right,' she soothed. 'He's not going to hurt you.' The reassurance seemed to bounce back at her and it sounded good. The warmth and smell of her dog was good too. Comforting. Anna raised her head to find that Luke was closer. He had dropped to a crouch and he was looking at the puppy.

'What is he, exactly?'

'We're not sure. The vet thinks he's about four months old. She reckons he's part poodle because of the wispy hair. Or maybe there's some wolfhound in there. A designer dog gone wrong, we decided, and that's why nobody wanted him.'

'A poodle and a wolfhound?' Luke seemed to

be making a valiant attempt to imagine such an unlikely combination.

He looked intrigued and, with his focus so completely on the puppy, Anna got the chance to look at him.

He looked so different. Was it the casual clothing or the fact that he was here, in her home? No. It was more than that. The grimness she was getting accustomed to in his face had lightened. The puppy had distracted him and caught his interest. Was it possible it might even amuse him? Make him smile?

Anna really wanted to see Luke smile.

'It could be possible,' she said, her tone deadpan. 'As long as they'd had a staircase handy.'

Luke's gaze flicked up. He gave a huff of sound that could have passed for laughter but there was no matching curl to his lips. Instead, there was an incredulous expression in those amazingly blue eyes. As though he was seeing someone he didn't recognise at all.

Because she'd cracked a fairly pathetic joke?

Or because of the reference to parentage? Canine sex.

Sex...

Oh, Lord! Anna closed her eyes. She couldn't hold the puppy any more tightly because she could feel his ribs too well already. Poor thing, he'd had a hard time in his short life so far. At least he'd stopped shaking, though.

'What's his name?'

'I can't decide. Every time I come up with one, I try using it but it doesn't feel right. Herbert was my last effort.' To her dismay, Anna realised that Luke would make the connection. That the surname of his first surgical case had seemed like a good name for her pet. How unprofessional would that seem?

Probably not as bad as talking about dogs mating on the stairs.

And did it really matter? This wasn't work. It was home. Different.

Confusing.

'He's got big feet.'

'Mmm. He's growing fast, too. I think that's why he's so clumsy. He got underneath my ladder and tried to turn around and that's how it tipped over.'

Luke was silent for a moment but then he looked at Anna and she saw that the grim lines were still missing from his face. There was a hint of amusement there but it was lapped by a sadness she could feel all the way to her bones.

'I knew someone once,' he said quietly. 'He grew too fast and looked a bit goofy, with his hands and feet always looking a bit too big for him, and he was such a clumsy kid we all called him "Crash". He grew up, though. Into the strongest, bravest guy I knew.'

He was talking about someone important. A fellow soldier, maybe? Someone he had loved who had died? Why was he telling her something so personal?

'I heard a crash,' Luke added. 'That's why I came inside.'

Anna swallowed. Luke's lips were moving.

Slowly but surely they were curling into a smile. A real smile. One that changed his whole face, deepening those furrows to his nose but adding a sparkle to his eyes that made him seem so much more…alive.

It faded all too quickly and instinct told Anna that she had been given a glimpse of something normally well hidden. The real Luke? A letting down of some guard that not many people got to see, anyway. A real smile and he had chosen to bestow it on her.

Something deep inside her was captured. Something huge and warm and wonderful. Anna knew she would remember this moment for ever.

'It's a great name,' she said softly. 'Crash?'

The big pup wriggled in her arms and looked up at her. He tried to prick up his ears but they were too heavy and stuck out sideways. Liquid brown eyes were full of trust and a long tail gave a thump of approval.

'Crash it is,' Anna announced. She smiled up at Luke. 'Hey, thanks.'

'No problem.' But the smile had well and truly vanished from Luke's face and he stood up.

He was leaving. Something oddly like panic made Anna's heart skip a beat.

'Would…um…would you like a coffee or something?'

'No. You're busy and I'm on my way to Penhally. I'll leave the journal.' He dropped it onto a chest of drawers by the door. 'There's a good review of restrictive pericarditis in there. I thought you'd be interested.'

The reminder of work was timely. She had to work with Luke. Work and home couldn't mix. Professional and personal couldn't mix. What had she been thinking, blathering on about her rescue puppy? She scrambled to her feet.

'Thank you.' There wasn't a thing Anna could do about what she was wearing or what her home looked like, but she could summon as much as she could of Dr Bartlett. Lifting her chin, she could feel the shell of professionalism beginning to enclose her. Protect her.

'That was thoughtful of you. I did do as much research as possible when Colin was admitted but it might well be something I didn't come across.' She looked pointedly at the door. 'I'll see you out, shall I?'

'No need.' Luke turned to leave but then paused. 'Actually, there was something else.'

'What?'

The hesitation was almost imperceptible. 'You don't seem to have reported that incident from Colin Herbert's surgery. Or not that I've heard about.'

'No. I decided not to.'

'Why not?'

'Because you said it wouldn't happen again.' *And I believe you*, Anna added silently, looking away so that he wouldn't see any crack in her newly formed shell. *I trust you.*

Luke didn't say anything. After a long moment he broke the eye contact and gave a single nod.

'Thank you,' he said, the words some-what curt.

And with that he was gone.

Anna stood very still. She listened to the sound of her front door closing. And then the sound of a car engine starting up and a vehicle moving away.

Even then she didn't move. Standing like this, she could feel that shell cracking and falling away, exposing something tender. She could almost feel Luke's presence still in the room. She could still see that amazing smile.

And, heaven help her, but she wanted to hang onto it for just a little longer.

The sound pierced his eardrums, his body rock-ing from the force of the impact. Through the painful buzzing that came in the wake of the explosion he could hear the cursing of his com-panions. The screaming.

'Get out!'

'Get down!'

The ping of bullets ricocheting off the metal of their armoured vehicle came faster. An unearthly shriek from someone who had been struck ripped through the sounds of chaos.

Of panic.

He could feel the heat now. Not just the normal strength-sapping attack of the desert sun but the kind of heat that could sear flesh. A lick of flames that could bring death with far more suffering than a bullet.

The dust was thick. Getting thicker. The chop-chop-chop of a nearby helicopter was stirring the ground. Bringing assistance, but it was going to be too late. It was getting hard to breathe. He could smell the dust. Taste it. Dust mixed with blood to become a suffocating soup.

His companions needed help. The driver was slumped over the wheel, others bleeding. The young paramedic was crying. Facing death and terrified.

He could feel that terror reach out and invade his own mind. He was frozen. Becoming aware of the pain in his own leg. Terrible, unimaginable pain. He couldn't breathe. Couldn't move…

They were his brothers, these men. All of them. And he was going to watch them die.

He was about to die himself. He could see the enemy emerging from the clouds of dust, their bodies shrouded with the clothing of the desert, their faces disguised by heavy, dark beards. He could see the cruel muzzles of the weapons they were pointing at him but he couldn't move.

Couldn't even breathe…

The sound of his own scream was as choked as the air around him.

Arghhh!

The desperate, strangled sound that finally escaped his throat was, mercifully, enough to wake him. Even as his eyes snapped open, Luke was throwing back the covers on his bed, swinging his legs over the edge so that it was a continuous, flowing movement that had him sitting, hunched on the side of his bed, his head in his hands as he struggled to drag in a breath.

The feeling of suffocation—of imminent death—was still there.

He couldn't afford to stay still. He knew what he had to do.

The warm, fleecy trackpants were draped over the end of his bed. His shoes were right there to shove his feet into. Running shoes.

It wasn't real, he reminded himself as he pulled the laces tight. It hadn't even happened that way. He had never seen the enemy. He had been able to move. To drag his companions to shelter behind the vehicle as the helicopter hovered overhead. He had staunched the flow of blood and kept airways patent. None of them had died.

But the nightmare was always the same.

He was watching his own brother die. Feeling the fear. Unable to help.

Matthew. Mattie. The clumsy kid with the

happy grin who'd had to tag along with his older brothers and do everything they did. Crash.

Oh…God! What on earth had possessed him to suggest that Anna Bartlett use that precious nickname for that skinny, ridiculous-looking dog?

What was she doing with a dog in the first place? How could she keep a pet that needed so much time and love with the kind of hours he already knew she put into her career? She did love it. He had seen that in the way she held it and soothed it. The way her face had brightened with joy at finding a name she really liked.

He had now pulled on the coat hanging by the door. Within seconds he was lurching down the rough track that led to the beach. It didn't matter that it was the middle of the night. His night vision was better than most people's and he was getting very familiar with this route.

Maybe it didn't matter that he'd given his brother's name away to a dog. It wasn't as though he was planning to visit that unlikely little cottage again and they were hardly likely to be chatting about it at work because they never talked about anything remotely personal.

In fact, he was having enormous difficulty reconciling the woman who was his assistant head of department with the person he'd found on the floor of that room cuddling…Crash.

Sea air so fresh that it bit into his lungs and numbed his face barely penetrated his awareness. He could feel the shifting of sand beneath his feet and hear the sound of the surf crashing in right beside him but his mind had fastened onto that picture of Anna on the floor.

With her hair in a soft tumble of curls. Her arms holding a vulnerable creature. Comforting it. Protecting it. He had felt the love. That was what had hit him in such a poignant place. What had reminded him of the kid brother who had never come home.

He'd reached the end of the beach now. Turned to go home again. He might even manage another couple of hours' sleep before daylight came. Usually, by the time he had done this punishing circuit, the nightmare had faded.

And it was only then that Luke realised he hadn't had to fight the remnants of that terrible dream the way he always did. From even before he'd left his house, all he'd been thinking about was Anna.

Or rather the two Annas.

Now that he'd seen her at home, he'd be able to recognise what he'd missed at work so far, surely? Some signs that hidden beneath that power-dressing, uber-professional, calm, cool and collected surgeon was…the most compelling woman he'd ever met in his life.

He was watching her. And he was puzzled.

Anna could feel the unasked questions hanging in the air between them.

Had it been real? Had he really found her wearing scruffy clothes, with her hair in an untidy mop, living in a shambolic house with a rather large and definitely unhygienic animal? Did she really have a sense of humour?

It was easy to emanate denial because that wasn't who she was at work. She'd also had years of practice in deflecting any line of communication that threatened to become personal. Patients could be so useful.

Like first thing on Monday morning when the anticipation of seeing Luke for the first time since he'd been in her house was making Anna feel more nervous than she had since her junior years as a doctor when she'd had to perform in front of some eminent consultant.

Luke hadn't looked any different.

'Good morning, Anna. How are you?'

'Very good.' She wasn't going to return the query. Luke wasn't one of her patients.

'How's—?'

Crash? She knew that was coming next and she had to stamp on that topic of conversation before it could start. The temptation to talk about her puppy was too strong. She wanted to tell Luke that Crash had learned to sit. That he had stepped on an overturned lid of a paint tin and made a giant pawprint on her wooden floor and it had been such a perfect signature she'd been reluctant to clean it off. Would that make him smile again? She couldn't afford to find out.

'Mrs Melton?' She interrupted smoothly. 'Finally getting to Theatre, thank goodness. I know it's your slot this morning but I'm more than happy to do the surgery. Or assist.'

'It's a long time since I did a CABG.' He knew exactly what she'd done in changing the subject. She could see him taking it on board that her private life was not up for discussion. Could see the focus as he let it go. 'Might be a good idea if you assisted.'

Was this a challenge? To see if she did trust him to operate safely on his own? A sideways glance as Luke fell into step beside her made her notice that his hair was damp. Just out of the shower? That image was disturbing. Anna dragged in a breath, only to catch a whiff of something fresh and clean. Like a sea breeze. Good heavens, she could almost imagine Luke had just been for a dip in the ocean. In the middle of winter? Who would be that crazy?

Her senses were threatening to override her train of thought. What had he asked? Oh, yes… Was he offering her the opportunity to observe and judge his capabilities in Theatre or might he want her company for an entirely different reason?

'I can't imagine that you'll have any problems,' she said calmly. 'But I am a little concerned about the quality of her saphenous veins. I'm wondering about harvesting the lesser saphenous or possibly upper extremity veins, in which case I could probably be more helpful than a registrar.'

Your choice, she threw at him silently. I'm available.

He simply nodded. 'Excellent. Have we got

time to review her films? I'd like to have a word with her as well and introduce myself.'

'Sure. I'm heading to the ward right now.'

Mrs Melton was thrilled to hear that the head of department would be doing her surgery. She beamed at Luke.

And he smiled back. Anna was watching and she could see that it was a purely professional sort of smile. It still softened his face and reminded her of when he'd smiled at her but it wasn't anything like the same. It didn't make his face come alive. It didn't come anywhere near his eyes.

She found herself watching him just as intently as she suspected he was watching her. She saw him smile in greeting colleagues. She saw him smile in satisfaction when he was informed of how well a patient was doing. He even smiled directly at her on one occasion. All mechanical gestures. Done because it was expected and it would be impolite not to.

Anna wanted to know what those shadows in his eyes were from and why they were dense enough to smother real smiles. She wanted to know who the real 'Crash' had been and why talking about him had cracked open the armour Luke wore.

For that was what it was. Anna could recognise it because she had her own. By the end of their second week of working together, she had the weirdest sensation that they were like actors. Playing their part on stage but with each of them knowing perfectly well that the role the other was playing was not the real person.

Even more disturbing, Anna was becoming obsessed with wondering about the real Luke. The man that had really smiled at her. Why did he come to work each day with his hair damp and smelling of the sea? The temptation to ask was becoming unbearable. Or maybe it was the desire to touch his hair...to press her face against it and see if that was where the impression of the outdoors and punishing exercise came from.

She wanted to know why he refused to admit that his leg hurt even when it was obvious it did. When there were lines of pain in his face at the end of a long day that she could feel herself. She could smooth those lines away. With her fingers. Or her lips. If he let her.

If she let herself…

The intrigue refused to go away. The pull became stronger but Anna was fighting it. Anyone seeing Mr Davenport and Dr Bartlett together would see nothing more than a purely professional association. Reserved but respectful. Discussions might be animated but they were only about their patients. Their work. Current research. New technologies. Endless topics to talk about.

A seemingly endlessly fascinating man to talk to.

* * *

If it wasn't for the puzzle that Anna represented, Luke might have been tempted to admit defeat.

Every day was the same. Enclosed within the walls of an institution that sometimes felt like it was filled with people who had created their own illnesses. Heavy smokers who seemed surprised that they'd had heart attacks because of their damaged blood vessels. Morbidly obese people who still expected lifesaving surgery.

What for? So they could carry on with their meaningless lives? Lie in bed and keep eating junk food?

'I'm not going to operate on Walter Robson,' he informed Anna after a ward round late that week. 'I refuse to spend my time patching someone up just to give them longer to indulge in slow suicide by their appalling lifestyle choices.'

If he'd hoped to get under her skin with such a terse and controversial statement, he was disappointed.

'I agree he's a poor candidate for surgery,' she said calmly. 'Maybe that will be enough of an incentive for him to stop smoking and lose some weight. If we can reduce his level of heart failure and get his type-two diabetes and cellulitis under control, it will reduce the surgical risk.'

Luke almost exploded. Thumped the wall beside them or walked away from his colleague. Told Anna what he was really thinking.

That she knew nothing about risk. Real risk— the kind that young, healthy people took for the benefit of their brothers-in-arms, if not for the much bigger human-rights issues. That patching them up was the kind of lifesaving surgery that had some meaning.

But that would open floodgates that had to remain shut. It would take Anna into a life that didn't exist for him any more except in his nightmares, and winning freedom from those nightmares was the hurdle he had to get through to survive.

He had discovered a new way of dealing with both the terrors of the night and the feeling of suffocation he could get ambushed by at work. He could distract himself by thinking about Anna. Just for a few seconds. Like a shot of some calm-inducing drug.

Her voice became a background hum as she talked about dealing with Walter Robson's anaemia and whether his chronic lung problems would improve if he carried through his vow to quit smoking.

Luke let his gaze stroke the sleek hair on top of Anna's head and then rest on the tight knot nestled at the nape of her neck. That clip thing would be easy enough to remove. The hair might still be twisted and squashed but he could bury his fingers in it and fluff it out until it bounced onto her shoulders.

His breath came out in a sigh. It was enough… the feeling of desperation was fading again.

'Luke?' Anna had caught the sigh. Fortunately, she misinterpreted it. 'The decision has to be on medical grounds, not moral ones.'

'Of course.'

This wasn't the place to discuss the ethics of what represented a significant part of their careers. Much of the workload was genuine and worthwhile. He knew that. He used to get more than enough satisfaction from it.

Why did everything have to be so different now? So difficult?

And why couldn't he see what he knew was there—hiding behind the person Anna was within these walls?

She wouldn't let him. That was why. The boundaries had been marked and were being reinforced every time she changed the subject if he tried to talk about something personal, like the puppy he had named for her. Or had she even kept the name?

No wonder James had sounded puzzled back on his first day when they had been scrubbing in together. As though he had no idea of what Anna was like out of work hours.

Maybe Luke was the only person here who'd had a glimpse of that side of Anna.

He liked that notion.

He liked it a lot.

CHAPTER FIVE

'I'M HAPPY to cover Christmas Day.'

'So am I.' Luke's nod was matter-of-fact. 'Thanks, Anna. That's the holiday roster issues sorted, then. Let's get on with the rest of the agenda.'

Anna couldn't help but notice the look that passed between James and Charlotte Alexander, who were sitting together in this departmental meeting. No mistaking the look of relief. Joy even at the prospect of spending a special day together with no danger of being called in to work.

The movement of Charlotte's hand was probably unconscious. She seemed to be listening carefully to Luke as he introduced a new grading system for cardiac patients.

'It's hoped that this will be brought in nationwide to try and standardise criteria and address the increasing numbers of people that are dying while on waiting lists for surgery. We've been asked to implement this at St Piran's as of the first of January as part of a multi-centre trial, so your feedback is going to be important.'

Anna was listening, too, but she'd already read the proposal and she and Luke had discussed it at length. It was hardly surprising that she caught that movement from Charlotte in her peripheral vision. A hand that gently smoothed the loose fabric of her top, gathering it up as it came to rest cupping her lower belly. There really was no doubt now that she was pregnant. It would be a special Christmas for them, wouldn't it, with the extra joy and dreams that came with knowing they were about to become a family?

'As far as degree of valvar dysfunction goes, we're staying with the New York Heart Association functional classes. As you can see, mild is class one and scores two. Severe is class three and scores fourteen. If there is coronary artery disease present as well, it puts it into class four and we can add ten to the overall score.'

Luke had the score sheets projected onto the wall. He was going to cover all the non-coronary revascularisation type of patients like valve replacements and then he'd run through the more complex scoring system for patients who had arterial disease. He was being clear and methodical and making sure everyone understood. People were nodding approvingly. A system like this could make prioritising people on the waiting lists much more straightforward.

Charlotte was one of those nodding. As though she would be only too happy to be filling in the score sheets on her patients and adding her comments to the feedback that would be required. But how long would she be around to be doing that?

It was all very well having secrets but it was also annoying. When were they planning to share the information and allow arrangements to be made for Charlotte's absence for maternity leave? For James to be covered at the time of the baby's arrival? For a new member of staff to be advertised for, if necessary?

No wonder there was such prejudice against women in top positions. Imagine if she was pregnant herself? Even if she worked up to the last possible moment and then took minimal maternity leave, the disruption to the department would still be huge.

Unthinkable. It always had been.

So why was she watching Charlotte surreptitiously right now instead of focusing on the information Luke was presenting? Wondering what her colleague was thinking and how she'd come to the conclusion that having a baby was more important than her career. What it might be like to feel a new life growing and moving within your own body. To face the enormous responsibility of caring for that baby when it was born.

The disturbing niggle was annoyance, not envy. Luke needed to know. He had quite enough on his plate settling back into running such a busy department and working the kind of hours he did with the extra stress of recovering from a major physical injury. Maybe it wasn't her place but Anna wanted to warn Luke. She could help him put arrangements into place to make sure they could cope with the inevitable disruptions.

Her gaze was on the head of department now. He was talking about the Canadian Cardiovascular Society's criteria for grading angina.

'The class is assigned after appropriate treatment, not at the time of admission or diagnosis.'

Luke stood tall but relaxed and his voice was clear and authoritative. What was the X factor in the way he presented himself that got people on side so easily? Anna found herself biting back a smile. It certainly wasn't his warm and friendly countenance. He was always so serious, often looking grim, and he could be down-right impatient with staff who couldn't get up to speed quickly enough. He was utterly closed off on a personal level and yet he drew everyone in.

Already this department felt more cohesive than it had under her own leadership. There was enthusiasm for all sorts of projects that might otherwise have been seen simply as more pa-perwork and stress. In the space of just a few short weeks they had a new rostering system in place, had been chosen for this pilot centre for an important national initiative and several new research projects had been kicked off.

Maybe that X factor was because of the sense that Luke was driven, despite—or perhaps be-cause of—the physical challenges it now in-corporated. Anyone could see how hard it was for him to be on his feet all day and keep up with such a demanding schedule. This job was his life and he was going to do it so well that anyone who chose to get on board would have an unexpectedly satisfying ride.

And she was one of them. Funny how the resentment she'd felt at Luke returning to take his leading role in the department had faded so quickly. Perhaps it had been pushed away completely because she'd been watching him so carefully and the more she saw, the more compelling this man was becoming. Had she really thought she wouldn't learn from him? It wasn't just his technical excellence in Theatre. Apart from that momentary wobble on his first day back, Anna hadn't seen anything that would have undermined her opinion that he was one of the best in his field. It was rare for someone so good on the practical side to be so competent at administration, but Luke really seemed to enjoy the challenge of running a large department effectively.

Yes. The closer she could stay and work with Luke the more she could benefit. She wanted them to be a close team.

How close?

The odd question came from a part of her brain that was normally closed off at work. The kind of disruptive thought that had never been a problem in the past but, curiously, had started to plague her out-of-work hours lately. She couldn't distract herself easily right now either. She was trapped, motionless, and she had already been distracted by the people around her.

'Scores for the ability to work or give care are a little more subjective,' Luke was saying. 'Especially the middle category when it's threatened but not immediately.'

Anna's concentration was certainly threatened. She didn't need a sideways glance at the Alexanders to remind her of married couples amongst her colleagues. It happened all the time. Didn't they say that you were most likely to meet the person you were going to marry amongst the people you worked with?

It wasn't going to happen to her. The desire

for a husband and family—if it had ever been there—had been dismissed long ago. About the time she'd discovered the passion she had for surgery and it had become obvious that if she was going to have any chance of getting to where she wanted to be, it had to be the only thing that mattered in her life.

Adopting a puppy had been extraordinary enough. A substitute baby? No. You couldn't leave a baby in the house for a helpful neighbour to collect and care for while you were at work. Or leave a pile of newspaper on the floor so you didn't have to get up in the middle of the night to deal with toileting issues. She still had to factor in collecting Crash every day from the yard he shared with June and Doug's dogs. To take him for a walk on the beach and spend time training and playing with him. To listen to the snuffles and odd whimpers in the night from his bed in the corner of his room. All in all, it was a major upheaval in her life. Not that she wasn't getting a lot of pleasure from it. And if it was a substitute child it was as close as she ever wanted to get, that was for sure.

No family, then. And what was the point of a husband if you weren't planning on having a family?

A partner was something different, however. A lover.

At this point in the meeting Anna very uncharacteristically stopped listening to anything being said around her. She was watching Luke's hands as he shaped the size of whatever it was he was talking about. Strong, tanned, capable hands.

She couldn't stop herself imagining them running down the length of her spine. It would be no effort to fit the curve of her bottom into their grip and he would be able to pull her against his own body with no more than the slightest pressure. It would feel lean and hard, like his face.

And he would have turned that blinding focus onto her. Those incredible blue eyes would be

on her face. On her lips as he dipped his head…
slowly…to kiss her.

Oh…dear Lord… With a huge effort, Anna
managed to tune back into her surroundings just
as the meeting was wrapping up. People were
closing diaries and starting to chat. Charlotte
pushed back her chair and stood up.

'Just before you all go…'

The buzz of conversation died. Here we go,
thought Anna, but the announcement wasn't
what she expected.

'I've been involved in organising the staff
Christmas function,' Charlotte said with a smile.
'It's in the canteen on the twenty-second, seven
p.m., in case you haven't seen the flyers. There's
going to be lots of nice food and plenty of non-
alcoholic drinks if you're unlucky enough to
be on duty. It's a chance for everybody to get
together in the spirit of the season, so I hope
you can all make it. Partners and families are
welcome. There's going to be a Secret Santa.
Bring a small gift and put it under the tree and

then you'll get one yourself at the end of the night. Or just bring one for any children that might be there and if they're not needed they can go to the children's ward.'

Anna looked away from Charlotte. Towards Luke. Their senior cardiology registrar should be talking about her upcoming maternity leave, not a Christmas party. Luke had an odd expression on his face. As if he couldn't believe that something so trivial was being announced in a departmental meeting.

As though a party or celebrating Christmas was absolutely the last possible thing he would have any desire to do.

Did he ever relax? Let his guard down and enjoy something social?

Something intimate?

She gathered up her folder of papers and stepped around the table. Towards Luke. She couldn't stop herself. The wanderings of her mind during the meeting might be under control now, thank goodness, but they'd left an odd kind of physical yearning and it was like a magnet, pulling her towards Luke. She did her best to disguise it. Her professional mask was quite intact, on the outside at least.

'Good presentation,' she offered. 'I think we'll have full co-operation in the trial period.'

'Yes.' Luke was shutting down the program in his laptop. 'I'm hoping so.'

Anna's thoughts were tripping over each other. She had a strong urge to engineer a way to spend some time with Luke and it would be easy enough if she asked to discuss something professional, like the planned research project she was taking on to analyse post-operative in-fection rates in cardiac patients.

But something new and rather disturbing was happening. She could actually feel the war going on between her head and her heart. She didn't want a professional kind of interaction. She wanted…

Oh, help… Was she actually thinking of asking him for some kind of a date?

No, of course not. She didn't do work relationships. Of any kind. This was Anna getting
rebellious, trying to claw her way through Dr
Bartlett's armour. It simply wouldn't do.

Her thoughts might be running with the speed
of light but she had been standing there for a
shade too long judging by the quizzical set of
Luke's eyebrows when he glanced up at her.

Anna was aware of the final staff members
exiting the meeting room, including Charlotte.
She hoped her smile was offhand.

'You planning to go to the Christmas party?'

'No. Are you?'

Anna couldn't look away. Her mouth wasn't
going to wait for her brain to mull over what
seemed to be a perfect compromise between
professional and personal. It just widened its
smile and opened to say something extraordinary.

'I will if you will.'

Something flickered in Luke's eyes.
Astonishment? Interest?

'I don't like parties,' he said.

'Neither do I,' Anna agreed. She could have left it there. What was wrong with her today? 'But this is a staff function. It's polite to put in an appearance. Especially for HODs.'

Luke was frowning now. 'You think I should go?'

'I think there must be a lot of people in St Piran's who would enjoy the chance to welcome you back. Good relations both within and between departments are useful.'

Luke grunted. He looked up as the meeting door swung shut behind the last person. 'Did you know Charlotte Alexander's pregnant?'

Was he trying to change the subject? 'I guessed. How did you know?'

'She told me. We need to look at possible replacements amongst the registrars we have available. Or get in a locum.'

'Yes. How much time have we got?'

'We should look at getting it sorted next month.'

'It's going to be a busy start for the New Year. Which reminds me…' The rebellious part of Anna had finally been quelled. Maybe it was just as well Luke was so good at sticking to professional. 'I wanted to have a chat to you about the parameters for this infection study. How retrospective do you think we should make it? I've got my registrar primed to start digging through records.'

'Let's have a look at our diaries. We should be able to squeeze in a meeting. You can bring anyone else you want involved along as well.'

'I will.'

Not that it was likely to help, Anna thought, her heart sinking. If she was capable of having totally inappropriate thoughts about her boss when there were a dozen or more members of the department around her, what hope did she have by flanking herself with a couple of junior doctors?

She needed to escape. To get home and get a grip. Heading purposefully away from work,

Anna barely registered the huge Christmas tree in the hospital foyer with its twinkling, coloured lights but she thought of it again as she turned her car towards her cottage.

This was the silly season, she reminded herself. Everything would settle down, including whatever it was that making her feel so...unsettled.

The Christmas party was well under way by the time Anna managed to get there.

The canteen was noisy and crowded, warm with the inviting aroma of hot, savoury food and people determined to enjoy themselves. There were bright balloons and streamers and huge, shiny silver stars hanging from light fittings. There were flashes of even brighter colours as well. Where on earth had people found their accessories?

A trio of nurses wore headbands with big yellow plastic stars that flashed on and off. Steffie, the staff nurse from the cardiology ward, had earrings and a matching necklace that had red and green twinkling lights. Anna spotted a set of glowing reindeer horns and Santa hats made of shiny red sequins. She passed a registrar who wore a large badge. Rudolph's nose was flashing and a tinny version of a Christmas song could be heard competing with the background carol music in the room. More than one person rolled their eyes as the owner of the badge reached to push the nose as the song finished.

'Not again, Peter. Please.'

A very young-looking nurse was dressed in a naughty Santa costume, the rim of white fluff on the bottom of her dress barely reaching her thighs. Anna groaned inwardly. This really wasn't her scene at all. She knew she must look as out of place as she felt. Prim, in her skirt and jacket. It was getting harder to respond to the smiles and greetings of people when she was completely sober and they were clearly making the most of the party drinks available to those not on duty.

She felt like an island. A rather barren, rocky one, moving through a sea of festivity. She had to be the only person there who didn't have at least a string of tinsel tied on to signal that they belonged.

And then she spotted Luke.

Another island. Even rockier, given the tight body language and an almost desperate look on his face as Anna edged through the partygoers to join the group of familiar faces.

'Anna. Merry Christmas!'

'Thanks, Ben. Hi, Lucy.' Anna smiled at Ben's wife, her gaze dropping to the bundle snuggled against the front of her body with a sling. 'I heard you'd had another baby. Congratulations.'

'Thanks. Yes, this is Kitty. She's ten weeks old now.'

A small girl was peeping out from behind Lucy's legs.

'This must be Annabel.' Anna searched her memory. 'It's her birthday soon, isn't it?'

'Christmas Eve.'

'Just as well she's a party animal.' Ben grinned. 'She's loving it.' He was holding Annabel's little brother, Josh, but he reached down to touch his daughter. 'Tell Dr Anna how old you're going to be on your birthday, darling.'

'Free,' Annabel said shyly. Ben tickled her head and made her giggle.

Who could help smiling at the joyous sound? Glancing up, Anna saw Luke's lips curve and it was, almost, the kind of smile he'd given her that day. Poignant. Real.

But not happy. The sound of laughter around them was virtually constant and Anna wanted to hear Luke laugh. To see and hear him forget himself in a moment of happiness. The feeling that he might never do that was heartbreaking. She tore her gaze away swiftly. Towards another smiling face.

But Josh O'Hara's smile looked forced and

the petite, blonde woman standing beside him wasn't smiling at all. She was draining a glass of wine.

The A and E consultant noticed the direction of her gaze. 'Anna? You won't have met my wife. This is Rebecca.'

Charlotte and James Alexander joined the group, along with another man whom Anna recognised as Nick Tremayne, head of the Penhally medical centre.

'Has anyone seen Kate? I told her to pop in while I was upstairs visiting my patient but I can't find her anywhere in this crowd.'

'Nick!' Ben stepped closer to the newcomers. 'So you got in to see Mrs Jennings?'

'Yes. The surgery went well. She should be up and about with her new hip in no time. Home for the new year.'

'How's Jem?' Anna asked. 'He was the talk of the hospital there for quite a while.'

'He's great. Started senior school in September

and seems to be loving it. Still gets a bit tired but it's been a big year for all of us.'

'Sure has.' Charlotte smiled. 'It's going to be a special Christmas this year. Your first together as a new family.'

'It's going to be wonderful. If I can find my wife, that is. Excuse me. Carry on enjoying yourselves. Oops!' Nick almost collided with a waiter bearing a tray of brimming champagne glasses.

Anna caught Luke's gaze and there was a moment of connection there. Neither of them was enjoying themselves in this setting.

It might be better somewhere else, Anna's response of a smile suggested. Somewhere without any of this crowd and noise. Somewhere they could be alone. Together. It had to be her imagination but Luke seemed to be silently in agreement. If nothing else, he certainly recognised the connection.

'Drink, Anna?' someone asked.

'No, thanks. I've still got patients I want to check on before I head home.'

'Definitely not for me,' Charlotte said happily.

'Or me,' James chimed in valiantly. 'I've climbed on the wagon with my wife.'

'Oh?' Ben's smile broadened. 'For how long, might I ask? Seven or eight months, perhaps?'

'Um…actually, there's something we probably should have told everyone quite a while ago now.'

The tray was still within reach and Josh's wife swapped her empty glass for a full one. Anna caught the expression on Josh's face. He's embarrassed, she thought in surprise. He doesn't want her drinking any more. No. The tension was deeper than that. It was hard not to get the impression that he wasn't comfortable having his wife there at all.

She took another glance at the woman she'd never met before. Rebecca had the kind of grooming that came, in her experience, with women who had plenty of money and too much time to spend on how they looked. Flawless make-up. Shoulder-length hair that was beautifully cut and exquisitely highlighted. Her nails sported a perfect French polish and her figure might be curvy but it looked well toned.

Rebecca had also caught the look from her husband. 'What?' she snapped. 'You think I've had enough?' A tiny snort suggested that an unhappy exchange was nothing new to this couple.

It was Anna's turn to feel embarrassed. She looked away to where Lucy was giving Charlotte a one-armed hug that wouldn't disturb the sleeping baby in the sling. Ben and Luke were both offering their congratulations to James and they all seemed unaware of the sudden atmosphere Anna was separating them from.

'Maybe I have had enough,' Rebecca said, too loudly. 'Of everything.'

'I'll order a taxi for you,' Josh said. 'I've still got some work I need to do tonight.'

'Of course you do.' Rebecca's laugh was brittle.

'Let's go.'

'When I've finished my drink. It's not as if I have any reason not to, is it?'

Josh's voice was too low for anyone but Anna to hear. 'I think we should go now. This isn't the place.'

'But it never is, is it, Josh?' Rebecca raised her glass but, to her dismay, Anna saw that the woman's lips were trembling too much for her to take a sip and tears were filling her eyes. Debating whether she should say something when it was obviously none of her business, Anna was relieved to see Rebecca blinking hard. Making a determined effort to control herself.

But then she shifted her gaze to where Lucy was standing with her tiny baby and Charlotte had pulled her top tight to show off her rounded belly, and Rebecca's face just crumpled. She pushed her glass at Josh and turned, tears streaming down her face as she fled. The others all turned in surprise.

'Oh…God,' Josh groaned. 'Sorry about that. I need to… Would you…?'

'Give it to me.' Anna took the champagne glass and Josh elbowed his way through the throng in pursuit of his wife.

'What was that all about?' Lucy looked worried.

'What happened?' Charlotte looked bemused.

'Josh and his wife. They didn't look very happy.'

Oh, no. Was this social occasion about to become the kind of gossip session Anna refused to engage in?

'Not everyone appreciates Christmas,' Luke said levelly.

'That's true.' Ben nodded and went along with making the subject about generalities. 'Look at the increase we see in A and E for things like self-harm.'

'The hype doesn't help.' Anna was more than happy to direct conversation away from colleagues and their probable marriage woes. She gave Luke a grateful glance and then waved her hand to encompass the party and all the decorations. 'There's this huge expectation put out that it's going to be the happiest day of the year. Brimming with fun, family times and the best of everything. No wonder it just serves to underline what some people aren't lucky enough to have.'

There was a moment's silence and Anna could have kicked herself. Had she been responsible for the atmosphere in this group going from joy at James and Charlotte's news to entirely unnecessary gloom? She bit her lip.

'I'm just hungry,' she said apologetically. 'Take no notice. I might go and find a sausage roll or something.'

'And I'd better take these guys home,' Lucy

said. 'We need to pace ourselves to get through all the parties lined up for the rest of this week.'

'And I…' Luke was obviously trying to think of a reason to excuse himself as well.

No surprises there. The noise level around them was increasing. Music had been turned up to compete with the laughter and happily raised voices, and there was a new sound mixed in with the general hubbub. A sharp cracking. People cheered and then there were more muted bangs. Someone was handing out Christmas crackers and people were pulling them with gusto.

The sound was not unlike distant gunfire. Anna's gaze flicked back to Luke. He didn't like parties anyway. How much worse would this be when it couldn't fail to remind him of being in a war zone? She could see his tension escalating. Instinctively, she found herself moving closer. Wanting to protect him. He looked straight at her and she had never seen him look so grim.

James was handed a cracker. 'Here we go.' He laughed, holding it out to Charlotte.

This bang was much louder. Charlotte squeaked in surprise, Annabel buried her face in her father's shoulder and little Josh burst into tears.

But Anna was still watching Luke. She saw the exact moment he stopped seeing her. When his face took on the same expression it had had in Theatre that first day. One of horror.

'Luke.' Anna put her hand on his arm and she could feel muscles as unyielding as steel beneath her fingers.

'Luke.' Her tone was more urgent now. She had to get through to him. Snap him out of this flashback before anyone else noticed.

But he didn't seem to feel her touch. Or hear her. He started moving away and seemed un-aware of the people in his path. Someone got jostled and spilled their drink.

'Hey! Watch where you're going.'

Ben and James were watching where Luke

was going. Anna caught the glance the two men exchanged. Frowning, Ben opened his mouth to say something but Anna shook her head.

'I'll go,' was all she said.

It was quite easy to follow Luke. People were stepping aside like a wave as they saw him coming. Smiles faded from faces to be replaced with dropping jaws. Anna didn't catch up with him until he was well past the doors of the canteen. She barely noticed Josh coming in the opposite direction. Good grief, this party wasn't proving very enjoyable for more than one person.

Finally, she got close enough to catch hold of Luke's hand but he didn't stop. He towed her along until he reached the end of the corridor. The noise from the canteen was muted now, like the lighting in this junction that contained the lifts. Two big pot plants on either side of a bench seat had some tinsel draped over their leaves.

Luke stopped and his head turned swiftly

from one side to the other. At some level he was making a decision on what direction to take next. He still felt just as tense. Just as distant.

Anna had to distract him. Bring him back to the present. She stepped in front of him and reached up to hold his face with both hands.

'Luke…' She tilted his face, forcing him to look down at her. 'It's me. Anna.'

He was still caught somewhere else. A long way away in time and place. Somewhere dark.

Anna had to do something. Without thinking, she stood on tiptoe, still holding Luke's face.

And then she kissed him.

CHAPTER SIX

LUKE knew that Anna was kissing him.

Just as he'd known that she had followed him from the canteen and had caught his hand. He'd heard the urgency in her voice.

But it had all been on another level of his consciousness. Maybe that was what it was like for people in a coma. Or coming out of one, anyway. They could hear the voices and feel the touch but there was a transition period before they were able to enter the same reality.

Something had snapped inside him with the sound of that cracker and he'd known he was getting sucked into a flashback. He'd tried to fight it off as he'd stormed out of the canteen. Tried to shut down the even louder cracks of the real gunfire he could hear. The explosions of landmines. The screams of dying men. But the pull had been huge. Even the smell of savoury food became acrid. Like smoke. Rusty. Like blood.

By the time he was in the corridor all Luke had been aware of had been the need to escape. To find somewhere he could be alone and bury his head in his hands until, somehow, he could wrestle the monster into submission and regain control. And then he'd felt Anna's grip on his hand and heard her voice calling his name.

He tried to clear his head. Tried so hard. He wanted to get back to her. He was caught in the horror of a battlefield and she was there but not there. If he could just reach her, everything would be all right. Couldn't she hear him shouting? That he was trying, dammit. Doing his utmost to get to her.

Maybe she had heard. Maybe that was why she was holding his head and pulling it down. Pressing her lips against his with such intensity.

God…he recognised this form of escape. Distraction. Release. An affirmation of life.

Passionate sex that carried no strings because if you got involved you only risked more of exactly what you were using it to escape from.

How did Anna know?

It didn't matter.

Luke could feel the force that had taken over his mind receding. He was in control again but instead of pulling away his lips moved over hers and his arms went around her body. He drew them both into the shadowy area between the bench and the giant pot plant.

He let his hands shape her body. Feeling the trim curve of her waist and the neat rounds of her buttocks and then up, beneath the layer of the tailored jacket. Up to the solid anchor of her shoulder blades and then around to the softness of her breasts. He cupped them and brushed his thumbs across the nipples that he could feel like tiny pebbles beneath the silky fabric of her blouse.

And all the time his lips moved over hers. Encouraged when they parted beneath his.

Excited when his tongue made contact with hers. Aroused beyond belief when she responded, her tongue dancing with his and her hands touching his body.

This was Anna, for heaven's sake! At work. The place where she had no personality or, at least, no personal life anyone was allowed to encroach on. Had she been drinking? No. She'd refused alcohol at the party because she had work she still needed to do. They were both sober. Sober enough to realise that this was totally inappropriate.

How long had they been standing here, locked in each other's arms, lost in a flash of physical release that had exploded like a cork from a champagne bottle?

Too long. Not nearly long enough.

Had anyone seen them?

He had to stop but it was too hard not to taste her for just a moment longer. To hold her against the length of his body and imprint the feel of her into his brain. He would need that memory and it was too important not to make sure that it stuck.

He was kissing her back.

Anna had only intended to distract him. A brief, hard kiss that was supposed to have the same kind of shock effect that a slap on the face might provide to someone in the grip of hysteria.

But after that first stunned beat of time he had kissed her back. His lips had softened and moved beneath hers and his hands had touched her body and something inside Anna had simply melted.

He hadn't seemed to hear her voice or know she was there as she'd followed him. Maybe he didn't actually know who he was kissing. She could be anybody so she didn't have to be Dr Bartlett, did she?

She could just be Anna.

An old version of herself, even. One that had

been lost too many years ago to count. The young girl who had dreamed of finding true love. A prince who was going to think she was the most wonderful person on earth. Who would love her for being exactly who she was. For ever.

And layered on top of that dreaming girl were flashes of everything she'd discovered about herself later. The yearning for a soul mate. The ability to give love and the need to receive it. Wild things like a need for physical release. All the things that had had to be buried so that they couldn't become a torment.

For just a few seconds Anna let herself sink into this astonishing kiss because she knew she would never experience anything like this ever again and she wanted to remember it, but the insanity began to fade and maybe she transmitted a tension that had nothing to do with desire. Something changed, anyway. She couldn't have said who actually broke the kiss and pulled away.

Maybe they both did.

For a long, long moment they stood there, still close enough to touch but not doing so. Staring at each other. Anna could see it was Luke looking down at her, not a tormented soul who was caught in a different reality. He knew who he was. Where he was.

And who he had been kissing.

Oh…Lord…

Anna swallowed hard. How on earth was she supposed to handle this? And not just the kiss. She'd witnessed another flashback incident. He'd said it wasn't going to happen again but it had. OK, so he wasn't in the middle of surgery and it hadn't endangered anyone, but there was no way her conscience would allow her to make excuses or ignore the implications of this.

She had a professional responsibility here and she had just complicated it to the nth degree by not thinking and by doing something as outrageous as kissing her new boss.

Then again…maybe that gave her a way in.

An opening to talk about what had happened and what they were going to do about it.

She took a deep breath.

'Feeling better?'

She knew.

Too much.

Luke could feel himself closing off. Slamming mental doors in an effort to protect himself. To protect her?

'Maybe I should ask you the same thing,' he said coolly.

'Sorry?'

'You kissed me.' He managed to sound off-hand, as though it hadn't blown him away. Like it hadn't meant anything at all.

He could see the way her eyes widened in shock as though he'd physically slapped her. The way she collected herself and looked away.

'You needed distraction.'

She couldn't know. Not everything. Not that she was already a distraction that he held onto every single night. That she represented a kind of rope that he could use to haul himself back to where he needed to be. A link that he had now tied firmly into the horrors of the past but one that led back to the present. To the future. A rope that he just needed to run his hand along to save his sanity. He would get where he intended to go eventually, as long as he could feel it running beside him.

The rope had been formed largely due to the intrigue that the contrast between what this woman was like at home and at work had sparked. Appreciating the fact that she was an attractive woman had woven another strand into it. But this…this blinding demonstration of what physical passion she was capable of did more than thicken the rope. It had come alive. It was warm and soft and he could stay glued to it with no effort at all. He didn't even need to touch it because a part of his mind could see it. Glowing.

'It was the Christmas crackers, wasn't it?'

Anna asked. 'That sound like gunfire. You had some kind of flashback, like you did that day in surgery.'

'Nonsense.' It was. It had to be because if it wasn't, it would mean he would lose his job and that was all he had to fill his future.

And if he lost his job, he would lose Anna.

'I didn't like the noise,' he admitted stiffly. 'I told you I didn't like parties. I left because I'd had enough. The noise of the crackers was just the last straw.'

'Do you actually remember leaving the canteen?'

'Of course I do.' And he did, in a vague, dream-like way. A background that had faded rapidly as he'd got sucked into the flashback. He remembered that Anna had been following him and… 'I…bumped someone,' he said aloud. 'They spilled their drink.'

That surprised her. 'You didn't look like you were aware of what you were doing.'

'I was…angry.'

'Why?'

'The party. The noise. All that food and drink and the silly costumes. It's all such a waste of time and money.'

She wasn't convinced. 'You didn't stop, Luke. You didn't hear me calling you. I kissed you because I couldn't think of anything else that might shock you enough to get you off whatever planet you were on.'

'And I hope you plan to include that little gem in whatever report you're obviously intending to make.'

A spark flashed in Anna's eyes. 'For God's sake, Luke. This isn't about reports or jobs or whether someone gets embarrassed. This is about the fact that if there's any chance of you "losing focus" or having a flashback or whatever the hell that was really all about that you're obviously not prepared to talk about, then you can't operate on people.'

Luke watched the play of expression on Anna's face. Her distress was all too easy to

see in the frown lines framing her eyes. In the
way her lips trembled.

'I'm not out to get you,' she said fiercely. 'I
want to help you.'

It was more than that, Anna realised as the
words left her mouth. Had it been growing
within her all the time she'd been watching
Luke so carefully? Hoping to see him smile?
Thinking so often about that short space of
time when they'd been alone in her house and
tumbling ever further into the confusion of her
response to him. She could see the shadows that
clouded his life and his eyes. There were things
that haunted him and closed him off but she'd
had a glimpse of the man he'd once been. Or
could be.

She wanted, more than anything, to dispel
those shadows. To get close enough to be allowed to help him.

She cared about him, Anna realised with
something like dismay. She couldn't pinpoint
when it had happened. Maybe the evidence had

been there for days and days. A sum of everything she had seen or imagined. Elements that
had floated in an uncoordinated fashion until
the fear she had felt in seeing Luke virtually
run from the canteen.

Something else had been added in when she
had felt him respond to her kiss. A confused
medley of caring and attraction. Not something
she wanted to try and analyse and she certainly
couldn't possibly tell him about any of it. Not
when it was beyond the realms of possibility that he could feel anything like the same
connection. Or that someone like him would
want help from someone like her. He was more
qualified than she was in so many ways. He
was older. More skilled. He had seen and done
things she would never want to do.

No wonder he was looking at her in a stony
silence that took a little too long to be broken.

'Help me?' The words were bitten out scath-
ingly. 'How do you propose doing that, exactly,

Anna? By spreading a rumour that I might be unfit to do my job?'

'No.' Anna tried to catch his gaze but Luke was looking at the blasted potted tree they were standing beside. 'I think if you have the time, you'll get on top of whatever it is or find the help you need from someone a lot more qualified than I am.'

The snort of sound was incredulous. 'A shrink, you mean? Cheers, Anna.'

She ignored the rejection. She'd be angry, too, if someone suggested she couldn't handle her own issues. 'What I was going to suggest is that you don't operate unless I'm assisting you. For the protection of everybody involved.'

'You think I need supervising? By you?'

Anna flinched, biting back the observation that he had needed her during Colin Herbert's surgery. Something told her that Luke was trying to turn this into a confrontation he could feel justified in dismissing. She had to find a way to rescue this discussion or she would lose him. For ever.

The lift suddenly pinged into life close by. The doors slid open.

'Oops, wrong floor,' a masculine voice said. 'Hey…sounds like there's a party going on.'

'Yeah. Staff do, mate. Doctors and nurses. Security wasn't invited.'

'Shame. Wanna crash it?'

'Nah. More than our jobs are worth. Come on. Push the damn button.'

The doors slid shut again but a single word of the exchange lingered in Anna's ears.

Crash.

The kiss seemed a very long time ago. Hard to believe it had happened, even. But it had and for a brief time Anna had felt the same kind of connection she had that day he'd told her about his friend 'Crash'. It was possible to find a chink in the armour he wore.

'Actually,' she told Luke quietly, 'I was thinking of it more in terms of it being beneficial to both of us.'

'So I get a supervisor. What do you get?'

'A mentor,' Anna said. 'The chance to learn from someone whose work I already respect.' She managed a smile as Luke finally made eye contact again. Had she also managed to placate him? 'Think about it. I'm going to go back to that party for a bit. I need some food.'

Going back into the canteen was the last thing Luke wanted to do but he found himself following Anna after a brief hesitation. He needed to prove he could. To Anna and to anyone else who might have raised their eyebrows at the manner in which he'd left. Most of all, he needed to prove it to himself.

He could see Anna walking well ahead of him.

He didn't need a babysitter. Or help.

He didn't need somebody kissing him because

they thought he was on 'another planet' either. Because they felt sorry for him?

No. Anna had said she could learn from him. That she respected his work. That didn't suggest she felt sorry for him. That kiss hadn't held any hint of unwillingness. Quite the opposite.

She'd kissed him because she'd wanted to kiss him. And what's more she'd wanted to keep on kissing him. It wouldn't have been difficult to pull away as soon as he'd responded. What she was saying was at odds with her behaviour. As much of a contradiction as her smart suits and paint-splattered old clothes. It was a puzzle and Luke liked that. He liked having Anna to think about. To ponder over. He was like a boat being tossed on a stormy ocean and Anna was his anchor. Maybe he could get to his future without her but it would be hard.

Lonely.

Luke was walking slowly. He could see the brightly lit interior of the canteen now, beyond the doors that were propped open by chairs. Anna had vanished into the crowd.

A couple stood on the shadowy side of the doors, partly screened because one of the chairs had shifted. A man and a woman. He wouldn't have taken any particular notice of them except that he could feel the atmosphere as he got closer.

A palpable tension. Maybe he recognised it because the air had the same charged feeling as it had had in those stunned moments after kissing Anna.

Sexual tension.

The man raised a hand to shove his fingers through his hair and then rub his forehead with the palm of his hand.

It was Josh O'Hara, Luke realised with astonishment. The A and E consultant he'd met the day he'd accompanied Roger into the emergency department after his cardiac arrest. The man last seen going after his distressed wife when she'd fled the Christmas party.

This woman was definitely not his wife.

She was quite tall and very beautiful, with long dark brown hair tied loosely into a pony-tail.

'I saw her leave,' the woman was saying. 'She looked dreadful, Josh. You should go home. Talk to her.'

'I know. I will. But she had gone by the time I got outside and I just had to... Oh, God, Megan...'

It was only a snatch of conversation that he overheard and Luke wished he hadn't. There was something going on and he didn't need to know about it. It was none of his business how difficult or miserable other people were making their lives.

He had more than enough to deal with in his own.

Something made him turn his head again, however, as he pushed himself back into the party.

He saw Josh move his head. Tilting it further

into the space behind the door that no one in here could see. Luke could sense the intent. Josh was planning to kiss this Megan. But almost at the same moment his head jerked backwards and he saw the shadowy figure ducking from reach as she emerged. She was shaking her head and she walked away without a backward glance.

Almost ran away, in fact.

That's what he should have done when Anna had gone to kiss him. Ducked the gesture and gone.

So why did he feel relieved that he hadn't even thought of doing so at the time?

Sleep proved elusive for Anna that night.

She couldn't close her eyes without thinking about that kiss and thinking about it brought it unerringly back to life.

She could still feel it.

The way his lips had moved over hers. Exploring them. Claiming them.

The strength in his hands. Their sure grip when he had pulled her close.

That incredibly gentle touch of his thumbs on her breasts.

And every time she relived that particular moment, her nipples tingled and a shaft of desire pierced her belly. And every time it got stronger. Feeding on itself. Taking on a life of its own. Becoming so intense it was physically painful.

With a groan, Anna shifted her body, turning over in her bed yet again. She had to stop thinking about it before day broke and she found herself on duty having had no rest.

Becoming aware of an odd thumping sound a moment later, she dragged her eyes open to find another set of eyes disturbingly close to her own. A long, wet tongue emerged to lick her face and the thumping accelerated when Anna laughed and wiped her face on her pillow to dry it.

'You're supposed to be asleep, Crash. On your bed.'

The puppy wriggled with delight at hearing her voice. He obviously had no objection to being awake in the middle of the night.

'It's all right for you.' Anna pulled her hand out from under her pillow and reached to stroke the dog. 'You can sleep whenever you want to in the daytime. I need to sleep now and I can't.'

Crash leaned against the side of the bed, his chin tilting up against the mattress.

'He made out it was all my idea,' Anna informed Crash indignantly. 'And maybe it was, to start with, but you know what?'

Big ears twitched into their endearing sideways position and Anna smiled as she stroked them.

'He liked it as much as I did, that's what. He could have backed off and he didn't. He kissed me back.'

And how!

Anna let her breath out in a long sigh. A release that was partly pure pleasure at the memory but it also held a good whisper of frustration and more than a hint of anxiety about the implications of it all.

Silence gathered around them both as Anna's thoughts drifted on the breeze of that sigh. Her hand stilled and finally Crash heaved a sigh of his own, folding himself into a lumpy shape on the floor. He didn't go back to his own bed. He was still there, right beside her, prepared to share any vigil.

But Anna's eyes had drifted shut. One thing was certain. That kiss couldn't be undone and it put her and Luke on new ground. Unexplored, potentially dangerous but undeniably exciting territory.

Was Luke awake right now?

Would he remember that kiss?

Oh, yes. Anna was as certain of that as she was about the fact that the kiss couldn't be undone. Curiously, the knowledge was comforting and sleep finally came, but it didn't quite erase the tiny smile curling her lips.

CHAPTER SEVEN

IF LOOKS could kill…

Anna had to bite back an ironic smile as she pressed her foot on the control to start the water flowing and reached for the small, soap-impregnated scrubbing brush.

She'd probably been glaring at Luke in a very similar fashion that first day they'd been in Theatre together. Resenting his presence. Resenting him. Knowing that she was perfectly capable of doing the job without him being there. Feeling demoted in some way.

Now it was his turn. This was his first theatre slot following that little talk they'd had after she'd chased after him out of the staff Christmas party. The issue had been ignored for the day or two since then. In fact, Anna had had the impression that Luke had been avoiding her and that had been fine because any embarrassment lingering from the kiss had been somehow watered down until it didn't exist any more. Maybe he was hoping she would also forget her intention of scrubbing in with him for the safety of everyone involved but she hadn't forgotten. She hadn't waited for an invitation either, she had simply arrived.

Luke was apparently focused on scrubbing his hands and forearms with commendable thoroughness. Under his nails and between his fingers. Carefully angling the water flow so that it chased soap from the wrists up to his elbows and then dropping his hands to rinse from the wrists to his fingertips.

He muttered something under his breath as he reached for a sterile towel to dry his hands. It sounded like, 'Blackmail'.

'Sorry?'

'Nothing,' Luke growled. He stepped towards a theatre nurse waiting to help him don his gown and tie it. He cleared his throat and raised his voice. 'Good that you had the time to join us this morning, Anna.'

'Wouldn't have wanted to miss it,' she responded calmly. 'Pretty complicated case. I'm sure I'm going to learn a lot.'

The nurse made an approving sound. 'We all are,' she said admiringly. 'The gallery's a very popular place today. Full house.'

Anna looked up and smiled at Luke.

See? the smile said. Nobody's going to blink an eye at me being in Theatre with you. We are the only two people who know the real reason I have to be here and we both know why it has to be this way. Her smile faded but she held his gaze. Get used to it, she advised silently. You don't have to like it but you do have to deal with it.

Not that she expected him to deal with it in quite the way he did. By making her the lead surgeon. Talking her through the more complex aspects but only taking over for a few minutes at a time. It was a long and complicated surgery. The middle-aged female patient had a tumour in one lung that had spread to send tentacles around the major vessels that returned blood to the heart. The diagnosis had not been made until the reduction in blood flow due to the compression had given her heart failure. Swollen ankles and shortness of breath had finally made her seek medical help.

Fortunately, they found no cardiac involvement, but the dissection needed to remove as much of the tumour as possible was tricky. The patient was on bypass for nearly five hours as Anna and Luke worked to free the blood vessels and remove a lobe of her lung. By the end of the procedure Anna was exhausted. It wasn't until their patient was off bypass and her heart was beating again effectively that she could relax at all and it was then that she realised how Luke had 'dealt' with what he'd taken to be her supervision. He'd made her do the work and put so much pressure on her that she hadn't had time to even think about how focused he had been.

If that was how he wanted to play this, it was fine by her. Brilliant, in fact. In order to watch her and challenge her to improve her own skills, he was having to focus just as intently as he would if he was doing the procedure alone. More so, in some ways, because he had to think ahead in several directions so that he could troubleshoot if she wasn't on exactly the same wavelength.

Not that any major discrepancies in thinking had occurred. They had been amazingly in tune. So much so that Anna would have noticed instantly if Luke had lost focus. He hadn't. She had been challenged. She'd learnt a lot. To outward appearances they had worked as a close, harmonious team. The initiative had been a huge success as far as Anna was concerned and not only from a personal perspective. The patient's quality of life had been improved immensely and, if she was lucky, the length of it might be well beyond current expectations.

While Luke might not be prepared to recognise it yet, there had also been an additional, albeit secret bonus. He had done more than save face. Nobody watching—and there had been plenty of them—would have thought there were any undercurrents. They would have seen a head of department using exceptional skills in both surgery and teaching. His kudos had probably been raised by several degrees.

She might be exhausted now but she was also delighted. This could work.

And maybe it was a good thing that Luke was grumpy about it. Anna found she was frequently the recipient of glares over the next few days. Surprisingly often, and not just when she might have expected to cross paths with her senior colleague on ward rounds or in meetings.

It was getting so that she could sense that brooding, intense look from a considerable distance. From the end of a corridor, for instance, when she got out of a lift. Or from across the canteen when she joined a lunchtime queue. He seemed to be everywhere. All the time. It didn't matter how late she stayed at work to catch up on paperwork or how early she arrived to get ahead with whatever her day held. He was always there. Or was it just that she was so much more aware of it?

Too aware.

So, yes, it was good that he was grumpy. It meant that he wasn't thinking about that ill-advised distraction of kissing him. Or, if he did think about it, it didn't make him happy. Either way, he wasn't going to want a repetition of anything like that and that was exactly what Anna needed to push herself forward. To get over it and get on with her career and her life.

It was good.

It was. And if she reminded herself of that often enough, it would be true.

It should have been a relief to get Christmas and the start of the new year over with.

To get back to business as usual and away from all the forced cheerfulness of so many people trying to spread the joy of the season. Even patients were wishing him a happy new year, and there'd been far too many invitations to social events to find plausible excuses to avoid. So many smiles to produce.

Theatre had been the best place to be, of course. No tinsel allowed in there and nurses had to remove any silly seasonal earrings. He didn't tolerate small talk either so he didn't have to hear people talking about how excited their children had been as they had counted down the sleeps or what people were planning to do to see in the new year.

The only downside of being in Theatre had been that Anna had followed through her threat of supervising him. His response had been a form of attack in a way. If she wanted it to be like this and pretend she was there to improve her knowledge and skills then she could jolly well put the hard yards in instead of watching.

To his surprise, Anna had embraced the perspective and anyone in the gallery would have been convinced that that was the only reason she was in Theatre with him. Even more surprising was how much he enjoyed teaching her. At some point during that first operation on the woman with that nasty tumour threatening her cardiac function, Luke had stopped watching like a hawk to catalogue things he could be doing better than Anna and, instead, began channelling his knowledge and watching how quickly she understood what he was saying and how deftly the information was put into use.

He not only enjoyed the session, if he was really honest with himself, it had also been a relief to have her there.

Just in case.

Having watched Anna so closely during that surgery, Luke found himself continuing to watch her. He justified the scrutiny by telling himself he was watching her to see whether she was watching him. He watched her on ward rounds and in meetings. Even in the canteen. It was easy to create any number of opportunities to watch his assistant. He could find patients in the intensive care unit whose condition needed review. Departmental issues to discuss. Research projects to plan and monitor.

He discovered that Anna spent almost as much time in the hospital as he did. Way too many hours to have any kind of life away from a career. How did she find time to work on renovating that small cottage she lived in or to give her pet the attention it needed? Not that it was any of his business.

Or was it? At one point, he had to wonder if Anna's willingness to put in so much extra time was purely due to her dedication to her career or whether it had something to do with him still being in some kind of probationary period. Was he just aware of it because he was trying to keep one step ahead of her?

Or…was he watching for a signal of some kind that she remembered that kiss?

That she might find herself thinking about it as often as he did? Sometimes he would catch her gaze and he'd feel an odd buzz. A hint that she might remember.

That she might be wondering if it would be as extraordinary if it happened again.

Wanting it to happen again...

On one of the first days of the new year, Anna was with Luke and one of her registrars in his office. They were discussing one of the new research projects due to get under way.

'The main causes of prolonged hospital stay, morbidity and mortality following cardiac surgery are haemorrhage and infection,' Luke was reminding the young doctor present. 'And, quite often, infection is one of the sequelae of haemorrhage.'

Anna was listening quietly. This was an occasion when she was in Luke's company but his attention was on someone else. Even when he involved her in the discussion, he would forget to glare at her and the simmering undercurrent that she was waiting on for further evidence that

Luke was unfit for the position of responsibility he held vanished. She could interact with—
and enjoy—the company of an intelligent and
stimulating colleague.

Bask in it even.

The registrar was nodding. 'Is that because
they're more susceptible to infection due to a
low cardiac output?'

'That's one of the parameters we need to keep
in mind. There's also the issue of how long the
chest has been open, whether they've been on
bypass or whether hypothermia has been em-
ployed. There's a lot of stuff that's been written
on aspects of this in other studies. What we're
aiming to do is possibly challenge their find-
ings with more current information or testing
methods and/or add in any other significant
parameters. Here, I've printed off some of the
articles for you.'

The registrar's eyes widened. So did Anna's.

How long had Luke been in here already
today to search out and print off this stack of

material? And this was supposed to be a day off for him. Didn't he have other places he wanted to be? Or other people he wanted to be with?

And why was the thought that he'd rather be here, having a meeting with her, a cause for a rather pleasant internal glow? Not that Anna was going to analyse her reaction. She didn't get a chance to, anyway, because her pager sounded.

The disruption earned her a sharp look from Luke and Anna sighed inwardly. 'Can I use your phone?'

'Of course.'

She found Ben Carter on the other end of the line and listened intently.

'I'm on my way,' she said a short time later. 'Luke's here as well. We'll both come.'

'What's going on?' Luke demanded as she put the phone down.

'Helicopter's due to land any minute bringing in a thirteen-year-old boy. He's hypothermic and unstable. Ectopic activity increasing so he could arrest at any time. Ben wants us on standby in case rewarming via bypass is necessary. He's put a theatre on standby as well and called in a technician.'

'You're the one on call. I'm not even supposed to be here today.'

Anna was at the door already. She turned to see the registrar looking slack-jawed at the potential case and Luke looking…good grief…wary? Or hopeful? Why?

She didn't have time to consider any personal issues. There was a child's life at stake here and if it came to trying to rewarm him by using cardiopulmonary bypass it was new territory for her. She'd read about it but never even seen it done. A flicker of something like panic had to be crushed.

She held Luke's gaze for a heartbeat despite— or perhaps because of—knowing he could probably see that flash of fear.

'But you are here,' she said quietly. The presence of the registrar in the room ceased to matter. 'And I need you, Luke.'

They both followed her but it was Luke's tall form striding beside her that gave Anna confidence. They moved fast enough for him to be limping by the time they reached the emergency department but they were still side by side.

A team.

The main resuscitation area in Emergency was crowded. Helicopter paramedics in their bright overalls and helmets were there with the medical staff, transferring their patient with great care. There was a bustle of activity and a buzz of urgent instructions.

'Gently! Don't bump him. Cardiac function is fragile.'

'Is the Bair Hugger on?'

'Dextrose, not saline. Get some more in the microwave to get warmed.'

'Make sure that oxygen is warmed and humidified.'

'Get some more dots on. We need a twelve-lead ECG.'

'What's his temperature now?'

'Nineteen point five degrees Celsius.'

Luke whistled silently.

'The lowest ever temperature that someone's survived without neurological impairment was around thirteen degrees, wasn't it?' Anna kept her voice low. The boy's mother was on the other side of the room, looking terrified.

Ben Carter was leading the resus team and he wasn't happy with the oxygen saturation level of the boy's blood.

'I'm going to intubate,' he decided. 'Anyone who's not directly involved step back a bit, please. It's critical we do this with minimal movement.'

One of the paramedics stepped well back, close to where Anna and Luke were watching. Standing by.

'What happened?' Anna asked.

'Kid got ice-skates for Christmas,' the paramedic said quietly. 'They live on a farm up north a bit and there's a dam. He and his brother went skating and he hit some thin ice and went through. Took his brother about thirty minutes to find a branch big enough to get him out and another half an hour to run home and raise the alarm. Probably ninety minutes before we arrived on scene and the wind chill was significant. First temperature we got was eighteen degrees.'

'Cardiac rhythm?' Luke was watching Ben and his team securing the boy's airway but he was listening to Anna's conversation with the paramedic.

'Slow atrial fibrillation. Marked J waves.'

Anything below a core temperature of thirty degrees was enough to put someone at risk of cardiac arrhythmias and arrest. This boy was dangerously cold but there was still hope. Anna remembered a lecturer at medical school talking about hypothermia.

'You're not dead until you're warm and dead,' he'd said.

The Bair Hugger was a blanket designed to force a current of hot air over the patient's skin. Intravenous fluids were warmed to try and raise blood temperature but these methods might be too slow to help someone with such severe hypothermia.

'Luke.' Ben had finally stepped back from the initial flurry of making sure their patient was as stable as possible. 'Didn't think you were on today.'

'I'm not.' Luke flicked a sideways glance at Anna and there was a hint of a smile on his lips. He was here because she wanted him to be but it seemed like he wanted her to know he was happy to be here.

'Well, I'm glad you're here. Both of you.'

'What's the plan?'

Ben looked grim. 'External exogenous rewarming is only going to achieve a rate of about a two point five degree increase per hour. He's

too cold to wait that long. With full cardiopulmonary bypass we could get a rewarming rate
of seven point five degrees an hour.'

'We can't justify something as invasive as
bypass unless he's arrested. What about pleural
lavage?'

The cardiothoracic registrar was looking bemused. Anna leaned closer. 'That's using an
inter-costal catheter to pour large volumes of
warmed water into the chest cavity.'

'Still pretty invasive,' Ben was saying. 'And
possibly less effective. Right now we'll keep
ventilator support going and monitor his
rhythm. We should get results on the bloods
we've drawn soon. I want to see what his acid-
base status is. At least slow A fib isn't a malig-
nant rhythm.'

'We need an arterial blood gas as well,' Anna
put in. She stepped forward to retrieve the sheet
of paper emerging from the twelve-lead ECG
machine but she didn't get time to analyse the

trace. An alarm sounded on one of the monitors at the head of the bed.

'He's in V tach,' someone warned. 'I can't find a pulse.'

'V fib now.'

'Start CPR,' Ben ordered, moving to the side of the bed. He looked back at Luke, who gave a terse nod.

'One shock. If that doesn't work, bring him up to Theatre under CPR.'

'Theatre 3's on standby. Bypass technician was paged when I called Anna.'

'Charging,' someone announced. 'Stand clear.'

Luke gave another nod and touched Anna's arm. 'Let's go. Better if we're scrubbed and ready by the time they come up if we're going to be needed.'

A cold, still heart.

This lad was technically dead and here they were thinking they could play God and bring him back to life.

Luke could see the lines of strain around Anna's eyes. He knew that her lips beneath that mask would be pressed tightly together. And, despite how subtle it was, he saw the way she flinched when her hands touched the chilled flesh in the small chest they had just opened.

'We need to work fast,' he reminded her quietly. 'Standard bypass. Arterial cannula in the ascending aorta. Right atrial cannulation with a single, two-stage cannula.'

Anna nodded. She was already placing a purse-string suture around the major vessel that took blood from the heart to the rest of the body.

Within minutes, with both surgeons working together in a tense atmosphere, the cannulae had been positioned and the boy's blood was now being circulated through the heart-lung bypass machine instead of his frail-looking body. Circulated and being carefully warmed.

There was nothing more they needed to do surgically until it was time to take him off bypass and repair the vessels currently holding the thick tubes. Then they would—hopefully—restart his heart, close his chest and wait to see if he woke up. Wait to see whether his brain function had survived this terrible insult.

Hours later, Luke found Anna in her office. She had been pacing back and forth between the intensive care unit and the wards. Between the canteen, where she'd eaten nothing at all, and the ICU. Between her office and the ICU.

'It's taking too long,' she said when Luke appeared through the door.

'He's in a good rhythm. Body temperature is within a normal range. The hyperglycaemia has been corrected. Renal function is looking good.'

'I know, I know.' But Anna was still pacing, her arms wrapped around her body as if for comfort. 'Blood gases are fine, too, and I'm happy with cardiac pressures. But what about possible complications like thromboembolism?

Or disseminated intravascular coagulation?' She dragged in a breath. 'Have you met his mum, Janet? Did you know his big brother is six years older and that she had two late miscarriages before Jamie came along? What...what if he doesn't wake up?'

'Anna...' Luke stepped in front of her, forcing her to stand still. He gripped her upper arms. She was so wrapped up in this case, so desperate for them to have succeeded, she was losing her perspective. He'd never seen her like this.

So involved.

Caring so much.

'The sedation is only being lightened slowly. It'll take time for him to start breathing on his own and he's not going to wake up before then.'

'But what if—?'

'Stop,' Luke commanded.

He was still holding her. Looking down at Anna's pale face. Those astonishing green eyes were locked on his. Hanging onto his words of reassurance. Believing what he was telling her. And then his gaze dropped to her mouth and he saw the tiny tremble of her lips and that undid something deep inside him.

'What you need, Dr Bartlett,' he said very softly, 'is distraction.'

She caught the meaning of his words as soon as he'd uttered them. Her gaze dropped to his mouth and he found himself running his tongue across his lower lip. Slowly. Deliberately.

Time came to a standstill.

'Mmm.'

The sound Anna made could have been agreement but it sounded more like need. Desire.

It was all the permission Luke needed. His hands left her arms. He used one to cradle the back of her head and with the other he cupped her chin. Then he bent his head.

He was initiating this kiss. He was in control and he intended to make sure Anna was aware of nothing but the sensations he was going to provide with his lips. And his tongue.

This was going to be a kiss that Anna would have no chance of forgetting. Ever.

Anna kept her arms wrapped around her body even after that first touch of Luke's lips.

She'd needed to keep hold of herself in those seconds leading up to that kiss. Feeling the way his fingers splayed and claimed control of her head and her chin. Sensing the intent of this being far more significant than the last time they'd kissed.

She'd kept her eyes open as she watched his face dipping to meet hers. So slowly. And she'd held herself even more tightly with her own arms then because she'd been sure she was falling.

Desire had sucked her into some kind of vortex and she was spinning wildly. Totally out of control.

And then his lips had touched hers and moved over her mouth. Questing. Claiming. Giving. Demanding her involvement and response.

Sensations rippled through Anna and unlocked the awful tension that had been building from the moment she'd touched Jamie's small, cold heart. Her skin tingled and seemed to melt and then her muscles gave up conscious control. Her arms let go of her own body and, instead, moved to hold Luke's. She could feel the strength of his muscles and the steady thump of his heart and all the time his mouth was doing such amazing things to hers. Her bones were melting now. He could just scoop her into his arms and lay her down on the floor of this office and she'd willingly—

Luke pulled away and for a dazed moment all Anna could think of was holding on more tightly. Pulling him back.

'Phone's ringing,' he said gently.

'Oh…' Anna put her hand to her mouth and took in a shaky breath. 'I—I'd better answer it, hadn't I?'

Luke was smiling at her.

Really smiling. His eyes were crinkled and

the corners of his mouth had disappeared into those deep furrows beneath his cheeks.

'Yes.' He nodded. 'I think you had.'

She actually stumbled moving towards her desk. Heaven only knew what the intensive care consultant on the other end of the line thought of her initial stammered response but the content of the call was more than enough to bring her back to the present and reality. She put the phone down a moment later.

'Jamie's breathing on his own,' she told Luke. 'He squeezed his mum's hand.'

To her horror, Anna felt tears gather in her eyes. She never cried. She most certainly never cried in front of a male colleague.

But Luke didn't seem to mind. He reached out and pulled her into his arms. Not to kiss her this time but simply to hold her. For long enough to be more than a celebratory hug. Long enough for Anna to know that he understood exactly how she was feeling. Long enough for her to take several deep breaths and get her brain working properly again.

'If we get up there soon, we might see him wake up and then we'll get an idea of what kind of neurological impairment he might be left with.'

An hour later they were part of the group around Jamie's bed in the intensive care unit as the young boy's eyes flickered open. His father and older brother were there now, too, but it was his mother who was closest. The first person Jamie saw.

He blinked a few times. Opened his mouth and moved his lips but his brow furrowed as though he couldn't find a way to make his mouth do what he wanted it to do. He stared blankly at the woman leaning so close to him, with tears running down her face.

Everybody present was holding their breath.

Luke and Anna were standing side by side. So closely their shoulders were pressed together.

Unseen by anyone else in the cubicle, Luke's hand moved just enough for his fingers to tangle with Anna's.

Jamie tried again.

'Mum?' The word was croaky but clear. 'What's the matter?'

Anna felt her hand gripped so tightly it was painful but all she moved was her head. Just far enough to meet Luke's gaze.

To see the triumph at the back of his eyes.

He let go of her hand before anyone could notice but that didn't break the link. It was still there in his gaze. A connection that had taken them way beyond being merely colleagues.

He would come home with her tonight. Or she would go home with him. It didn't matter. It wasn't even a decision that needed to be discussed because it had already been made. Back in her office. Or maybe well before that but neither of them had taken that step forward.

Now they had taken that step and they both knew there was no going back.

CHAPTER EIGHT

CRASH stayed at the farm up the road from Anna's cottage.

'He often does,' she assured Luke. 'That way I don't disturb the Turners by collecting him if I have to work late. June loves him to bits. She would have kept him except that Doug put his foot down.'

She was talking quickly, Luke noticed, as the glow of realising she had kept the name he'd suggested for her puppy wore off. Was she nervous? Unsure she was making the right choice here, a passenger in his car as they drove away from St Piran's hospital that evening?

He was feeling a bit uptight himself. Sex in an army camp was a lot easier than this. You got attracted or desperate for distraction and a tent or somewhere private was never far enough away to allow for second thoughts. No awkwardness. No pressure. No strings afterwards.

This was different.

There was danger here. For the peace of mind he was struggling to achieve. For the relationship with an important colleague that could get damaged. And for Anna...because she might get hurt. She might want something that he couldn't give her.

Like commitment.

Curious that the prospect of hurting Anna outweighed the more personal ramifications this step could represent. He wanted to protect her. To turn his vehicle round and take her back to the hospital. Let Anna drive home to her small cottage. Alone.

Luke flicked a sideways glance at his passenger as he turned onto the road that led to his beachside house. She'd pulled out whatever it was she used to restrain her hair and it tumbled to her shoulders. Her hands were clasped in her lap and she was still wearing her power-dressing clothes.

Not for long, though. Luke found he had to lick suddenly dry lips. There was still time, he told himself. He could turn round. Tell her that he'd changed his mind and maybe this wasn't such a good idea after all, given how closely they needed to keep working together.

But Anna seemed to sense that quick glance and she turned her head as well. Her eyes seemed huge in a pale face as they drove under a streetlamp. Her lips were parted a little and maybe she was experiencing the same kind of dry mouth he was because she mirrored his own action and licked her lips. The action rendered Luke helpless to act on any good intentions. Almost ashamed of himself, he cleared his throat and it came out in a kind of growl.

Anna sighed, assuming the sound was related to the conversation she was using to fill the awkward journey.

'I know, I was crazy to take on a puppy with

the kind of hours I have to work but when I am at home he's wonderful company.'

Oh, God…was she lonely?

The urge to protect this woman from being hurt morphed into something very different. He might not be able to offer commitment or any kind of a future but he could step, temporarily at least, into that void in her life and give her some companionship. The kind of closeness that would make her feel like she wasn't alone in the world. That someone cared enough to give her pleasure.

That someone cared at all.

She wasn't the only one here who needed that.

Anna was pleased that Luke didn't draw the curtains in the bedroom he led her into. His house was almost on a beach. Not one of the rocky, dangerous coves that dotted this coast but a sandy stretch with enough width for smooth waves. The kind of gem tucked amongst the rocky ones that surfers loved to try and keep secret. She could see it because it was a clear, cold night and there was enough moonlight to not only show her the view but to mean that harsh electric lighting was unnecessary inside. That pleased her, too.

She had already declined an offer for any food or drink. That could come later. Or not. They were there for one reason and that was to continue the kiss that had begun in her office. To finish what had been started.

Standing here was different, however. Anna was too nervous to look at the bed so she stood in front of the big window that had the view of the beach and stared out. Luke came to stand very close behind her. His hands brushed her arms. A slow stroke from her elbows to her shoulders and back again and there his hands lingered.

'Are you sure about this, Anna?' he asked quietly. 'It's OK if you want to change your mind.'

She turned and it was suddenly very easy.

As though his body warmth was an irresistible magnet. Her breast brushed his hand as
she moved and the sensation blitzed any final
nerves.

'I don't want to change my mind,' she said
softly. 'Do you?'

By way of response, Luke bent his head and
his lips touched hers. The chill of the evening
outside was coming through the uncovered
glass beside them and the pale light of the moon
offered no pretence of warmth, but Anna had
never felt heat like this.

Scorching her lips as Luke claimed her mouth.
Trickling over her body with the touch of his
hands as he undid the buttons of her blouse and
undressed her. Building inside as she watched
him strip and stand there, bathed in moonlight.
Tall and lean and powerful. Magnificently male.

She wanted him to catch her in his arms and
throw her onto the bed but, instead, he came to
stand in front of her. Skin to skin. Her breasts
pressed into the hardness of his chest and she

could feel his arousal against her belly. He wanted her. As much as she wanted him. His arms came around her then and their lips met. In a kind of slow dance, moving as one person, they somehow made their way from the window to the bed and then they were lying together. A tangle of limbs and passionate kisses and a consuming need that brooked no delay other than Luke fishing in a bedside drawer for protection.

The few seconds of watching him was like being suspended in time and space for Anna. The piercing anticipation had to be the most delicious sensation she had ever experienced and she clung to it, knowing that it would end very soon. Wanting it to end so that she could feel Luke inside her. Touching parts of her body that had never felt so hollow. Reaching places that weren't even physical.

She just knew he would be able to touch her soul.

Passion so intense had to explode and burn out in a dramatic climax and if that had been the end of it, it would have been incredibly satisfying on a physical level. Even better was that Luke smiled at Anna when they finally caught their breath.

'Now we can really get to know each other,' he promised.

And they did. A slow exploration of each other's bodies. A shaping of muscles on Anna's part with a compliment on how fit he must be. A tracing of Anna's breast with a single finger that ran across the flatness of her stomach to her belly button.

'You are beautiful,' Luke told her.

She found the scars on Luke's leg and he tried to move her hand but she resisted.

'They're part of you, Luke,' she said gently. 'Don't hide. Please.'

He went very still as she touched the misshapen muscle of his thigh and the lumpy ridges of the scars.

'Ugly, isn't it?' he ground out finally.

'No. They tell me that you have courage. That

you're different.' Anna propped herself up on one elbow to look down at Luke. Even in this half-light she could see the shadows in his eyes that were part of the scars she had just been touching. What she could feel on his leg was nothing compared to the scars that had to be still hidden.

'Special,' she added in a whisper, leaning down to kiss him. She tried to put what she couldn't put into words into that kiss. To tell him that she accepted him for who he was. With scars. That she had courage too. That she could be trusted.

They made love again and this time it was slow and sweet and, in its wake, Anna fell asleep in Luke's arms, drifting off in a cloud of utter contentment. Of promise. Of a hope so compelling it was safer to go to sleep than con-template the notion that it might be unjustified.

She woke some time later to find herself alone in a strange bed. She lay there, listening, but the house had that peculiar kind of silence that told her she was alone within these walls. Turning her head, she caught the glow of a digital, bedside clock. It was 3 a.m. Where on earth was Luke?

Taking the rumpled sheet with her to wrap around her body, Anna climbed from the bed. Instinct took her straight to the window and she stared out, the way she had when she'd first entered this room. For a long minute it was too dark to see anything. Then the moon emerged from thick cloud and she saw him. On the beach.

Running.

How could he be doing that? Not just because it was the middle of the night and it had to be well below zero out there, but how hard would it have to be to do that, in soft sand, on a leg that was damaged enough to make him limp at a fast walking pace or put him in noticeable pain when he had to stand for any length of time?

He was more driven than Anna had suspected and it was disturbing. Maybe he wasn't driving himself towards something. Maybe he was trying to run away.

He came back to the bed a while later, warm and fresh from a hot shower, and when he reached for Anna, she was happy to sacrifice further sleep to make love yet again. This time, however, there was an edge that hadn't been there before. Concern for Luke. The knowledge that she was with a deeply troubled man.

When daylight broke, Luke was absent from the bed again but Anna knew where to look. He wasn't running on the beach this time. She could see the dark shape striding into the surf. Diving into a breaking wave further out and then surfacing to swim, with a strong, steady stroke, parallel to the sand.

She had showered and dressed by the time Luke returned to the house. She saw him coming up the path in his wetsuit, carrying dripping flippers in one hand. His face registered surprise.

'You're not going to stay for breakfast?'

'I'd better not. I need to collect Crash and I've got a huge list of things I want to get done on my day off. If I can finish the painting and get the windowsills sanded and varnished, I can put my bedroom back together properly tonight.'

'Shall I come over after work and give you a hand?'

Anna hesitated. She could decline the offer and send a signal that she wanted to slow down whatever was happening between them. If she accepted, it would take them to a new level. The start of a relationship instead of a one-night stand.

Luke was pulling the zipper on his wetsuit. Peeling it away to reveal his bare torso, and Anna's body instantly reminded her of exactly what it had felt like to have those hands peeling away her own clothing. The sound of the nearby surf reminded her of watching him in the night, punishing his body by pounding over the sand. Enduring the pain in his leg because he was driven. And courageous.

And she…loved him for it?

Oh, help!

'I—I'd love a hand,' she heard herself say aloud. Good grief, what was she doing? She couldn't stop herself. 'I'll cook you some dinner. Do you realise we totally forgot to eat last night?'

Luke looked more surprised than he had on finding her dressed and ready to leave.

And then he smiled. 'Sometimes food can be overrated. I had everything I needed.'

Anna actually blushed as she smiled back. 'Me, too.'

A day at home was important for Anna.

By throwing herself into the renovations of her cottage and spending time playing with Crash, she could banish Dr Bartlett and let her recharge her professional batteries. Usually the door between work and home was firmly closed but today there was a wedge preventing that. She found herself wondering where Luke might be and what he might be doing.

He wouldn't be in Theatre. Although the tacit agreement that they would act as a team for surgery was still new, it was working and Anna trusted Luke not to break it. If something extraordinary happened, like Jamie's case had presented yesterday, he would call her in.

How was Jamie today? Anna peeled off her gloves and discarded the sandpaper she had been using, intending to make a call, but the phone rang as she walked towards it.

'I thought you might like an update on Jamie,' Luke said. 'We're transferring him to the ward this afternoon. He's bouncing back from his surgery remarkably well and I think we'll find he'll end up showing little effect from being virtually frozen to death.'

Anna listened to Luke's voice and absorbed the welcome news. The call ended, she went back to varnishing her windowsill. Thoughts of Luke were there as pervasively as the smell of polyurethane. Catching sight of Crash ripping her sandpaper to shreds with his tail thumping, she made a mental note to get to the supermarket so that she had something to feed Luke for dinner tonight. What did he like to eat? What would he like to do when they'd finished eating?

Oh, Lord. She could only hope that Luke wasn't in his office, struggling to concentrate on important paperwork, getting ambushed by memories of their astonishing night together. On the other hand, maybe she hoped he was. This was all as confusing as it was wonderful.

She put a roast of beef in the oven to cook slowly and fill her cottage with a welcoming aroma. She wanted Luke to feel welcome. She purchased wine, too. She wanted him to relax and feel comfortable. This was another new step. A chance to get to know each other better on more than a physical level. A chance to talk about things other than work. A chance to test these newborn feelings she was experiencing. To see if there was a chance of finding ground that might nurture them or whether they needed to be ruthlessly weeded out.

Except that turned out to be harder than Anna had anticipated. Luke seemed happy to be in her home and he clearly appreciated the meal, though he declined any alcohol. He was polite but unforthcoming when it came to any personal conversation.

'What was it like?' Anna asked at one stage. 'Working in a field hospital?'

'Basic. Fast and bloody.' His tone was detached enough to signal a lack of desire to go into details. 'These Yorkshire puddings are fantastic,' he said into the moment's silence that fell then. 'Where did you learn to cook like this?'

'My mother was adamant that a girl had to be able to cook. So was my father, come to that.'

'And you weren't.'

It was a statement, rather than a question. Delivered with a quizzical edge that made Anna think he could see right into places in her heart that even she didn't peer into too deeply any more.

'Things that boys were allowed to do were

more important. I jumped through the girl hoops but it wasn't enough.' Anna looked down at her plate. 'My father wanted a son that he never got.'

She heard Luke's fork clatter as he put it down. Then she felt him touch her hand. 'He got something better, then, didn't he? They must be very proud of you.'

Anna shrugged. 'Surprised might be closer to the mark. Disappointed, maybe, that I didn't become a teacher or a nurse and shower them with grandchildren. Grandsons,' she amended with an attempt to lighten the revelation with a smile. 'What was your family like, Luke? You weren't an only child, were you?'

'No. All boys in my family but if there had been a girl she would have been expected to do the boy things. She wouldn't have had a choice, really, being dragged from one military post to another. I was the one to break the family tradition and become a doctor instead of a soldier.

Even then, I was expected to aim for a career as an army medic. I rebelled.'

'You went in the end. I'm sure your parents are proud.'

'They're in New Zealand,' Luke said, as though that answered the unspoken question. And then he steered the conversation away from himself again. 'What's the next project you've got lined up for the cottage?'

He helped her clean up after the meal and then he helped her move the bedroom furniture back into place. And then, as Anna had hoped he would, he took her into her own bed and made love to her. He wouldn't stay the night, however.

'I've got so much reading to catch up on,' he excused himself in the early hours. 'You've got no idea how out of date you can get by taking a year or two off. I've got to keep up my exercise program, too, and I can't miss my early swim.'

Too many good reasons not to stay.

'Don't you ever sleep, Luke?'

'Sleep's overrated.' He bent to kiss Anna again as he took his leave. 'Life's too short to waste it.'

Maybe sleep wasn't so overrated.

Fatigue was like a form of anger. Something that simmered and bubbled occasionally to splash in unexpected directions.

'That is a surgical mask, not a damned bib. Don't come into this theatre unless you're going to wear it properly.'

The junior theatre nurse went pale and fled. Luke looked away as Anna glanced up from the meticulous stitches she was placing in preparation for a mitral valve replacement. He knew there had been no real reason to snap at the nurse. She'd been delivering some new IV fluid supplies, not planning to come and lean over the operating table.

'I've got all the anular sutures placed and tagged,' Anna said.

'Let's get the valve seated, then, and tie them off.'

'OK,' Anna said as the procedure continued. 'I'll have the aortic needle vent now, thanks.'

Luke watched as she removed more air and then restarted the heart.

'Can you elevate the apex of the left ventricle?' she asked him. 'If those adhesions are too dense, I'll go for clamping the aorta. I'd like to follow up with an echocardiograph to check.'

Would she say something when this was over? Reprimand him in some way for his irritation with the junior nurse? He probably deserved it, given that this wasn't the first time.

Ripping off his mask and the disposable hat as he left Theatre, Luke pushed his fingers through his flattened hair. What was wrong with him?

It wasn't simply fatigue. Insomnia had been a part of his life for many months now and he had coped. Maybe the difference was that he was choosing to stay awake when he craved sleep.

Night after night. It had been nearly a week now. He would hold Anna in his arms after they'd made love and feel the way her body softened and her breathing slowed. The blissful temptation of sleep would pull at him in those moments, too.

Taunt him.

When he needed sleep and was ready for it, it wouldn't come. If offered itself at times like this, when he couldn't accept. He just couldn't go there because he had no control over what his sleeping mind chose to do. While it could be the saving of him to have Anna to hold close in the wake of a nightmare, he had to spare her from sharing that part of his life, because then he'd have to talk about it and he wasn't going to do that with anybody.

If he could bury it, it would go away.

Eventually.

Luke fell asleep the next night Anna stayed at his house.

Maybe that was what had woken her—the

change in how he was holding her. It was more like she was holding him right now. With a careful tilt of her head, she could see his face and it looked so different she was shocked. He looked so much younger. Unguarded.

Vulnerable.

Those piercing, intense eyes were shuttered. His lips were soft and slightly parted and she could hear his soft, even breaths. Even the furrows at the top of his nose had softened. Anna willed herself not to move. She didn't want to wake him. Heaven knew, he needed the sleep. Nobody could keep up the kind of pace Luke did without coming to physical harm. It was no wonder he snapped at the people around him occasionally.

So she stayed awake. Holding this man she was coming to feel more deeply for every day. Wanting to protect him and give him the healing rest that only sleep could provide. That was probably why she felt the moment the nightmare started. The way the muscles beneath her hands and arms became so tense. She could hear the way his breathing became shallow and rapid. His heart was pounding beneath his ribs and she could feel the rumble of his moan even before it reached his lips.

'No-o-o-o…'

'Luke. Wake up.' Anna held him more tightly. 'It's all right. It's just a bad dream.'

She couldn't hold him now. The strength in his body was frightening as he twisted and fought whatever demons had come in his sleep. Anna could see the sheen of sweat on his body. His breath came in choking gasps now—as though he was suffocating.

'Arghhh!' The sound was one of agony.

The covers were hurled back from the bed and Luke swung his legs over the side. He was almost crouching there and he covered his face with his hands.

Anna scrambled to her knees and across the bed. Kneeling behind Luke, she wrapped her arms around him.

'It's all right,' she said, hoping her voice wouldn't betray how shaky she was feeling. 'I'm here, Luke. You had a nightmare.' That's all, she wanted to add, but bit the words back. This wasn't something that should be belittled in any way.

His breathing was slowing now. For a moment he leaned back into Anna's embrace but then he lurched to his feet.

'I need some fresh air,' was all he said. He began dragging on clothes. Fleecy track pants. Running shoes.

She couldn't make him tell her anything about the nightmare if he didn't want to. Anna closed her eyes. Waiting. Hoping.

'You...' Luke paused as he got halfway across the room but he didn't turn round. 'You weren't... I didn't want you to see that.'

'It was a nightmare, Luke. Don't go. You don't have to run away from it.'

The huff of sound from him was angry.

She knew nothing. And he wanted it to stay that way.

'Would you rather I went home?'

'Up to you. I won't come back to bed. I've got some work I may as well do now that I'm awake. After my run.'

And with that he was gone.

Anna didn't want to wait. There was no moon tonight so she wouldn't be able to see him down on the beach. She didn't want to watch either. Luke had his own way of dealing with whatever was bothering him and it didn't include her.

What was she to him? With a sinking heart Anna found her clothes and then the keys to her car. Was this just about the sex?

Distraction?

When she arrived home to her cold cottage, Anna put an electric heater on and made a pot of tea. It was nearly 4 a.m. and she was far too wound up to go to sleep again. She missed Crash.

Opening her briefcase, she got her laptop out

and connected to the internet. With no emails that caught her interest, she idly clicked on a search engine and stared at the flashing cursor.

'PTSD', she tapped in on impulse.

So many sites. She opened the one that had been given first place in the queue and within minutes she was totally engrossed.

Post traumatic stress disorder was a syndrome that could develop following any traumatic event. Things like natural disasters and car crashes, violent assaults or even medical procedures, especially for children. Top of the list, however, as she'd known quite well, was war.

Traumatic experience put the mind and body into a state of shock, she read, but most people could make some sense of what had happened, process the resulting emotions and come out of it eventually. In PTSD, the person remained in psychological shock. There was a disconnection between the memory of the event and how the victim felt about it.

Anna read on, almost feverishly, skipping a few paragraphs to the heading of 'Symptoms'.

Nightmares.

Flashbacks.

Difficulty falling or staying asleep.

Irritability or outbursts of anger.

She found herself nodding at that one. She hadn't said anything about the way Luke had snapped at that poor theatre nurse the other day but other people were talking about it. And about the way he had avoided all social invitations outside the hospital over the Christmas and New Year period. Some were keen to remember his odd behaviour at the one event he had attended and the way he'd stormed out of the canteen.

Her eyes drifted further down the list. Not that she needed any more information to confirm what she was already convinced of.

Depression was common. So was guilt. People often attempted to numb themselves through substance abuse. Luke obviously avoided drinking but wouldn't his exercise regime fit into the same category? How numb would you get, running or swimming in the middle of winter? And physical pain could override mental suffering.

The victim could also feel detached from others and emotionally numb. They would have a sense of a limited future and wouldn't expect to live a normal life span or get married and have a family. PTSD would harm relationships, the ability to function and their quality of life.

There were treatments suggested, of course, but they came with the background rider that the sufferer had to be willing to confront it and not see the admission as a sign of weakness. Luke had been brought up in a military family. Was it the kind of thing that didn't get mentioned? That he wouldn't be able to allow himself to admit? He'd denied having flashbacks. Pushed her away in the wake of that nightmare. He 'hadn't wanted her to see it'. Had he ever, in fact, gone to sleep before when she'd been in the same bed?

Maybe her intrusion into his personal life was making it worse. Removing opportunities he might have otherwise had to sleep. Putting stress on him by making him think he had to factor her into a future that might already seem too difficult.

It was so clear to her that Luke was suffering from PTSD. It was also very clear that the only way to conquer it was to confront it. Somehow he would have to learn to accept it as part of his past. Numbing it or pushing the memories away would only make it worse and it was more likely to emerge under stress.

The sound of a distant beeping finally intruded on Anna's thoughts and she realised her alarm clock was going off. Her huff of laughter was ironic. It was time to get up and get ready for work. With a heavy heart she went through the motions, but she couldn't stop thinking about the pieces that had finally fallen into place and created a picture so much darker than she had feared.

As far as she was concerned, she was a part of that picture. She was in far too deep to escape. She didn't want to.

For better or worse, she had fallen in love with Luke Davenport.

She wanted to help him.

But how?

CHAPTER NINE

'WHAT'S this?' Anna had stooped to pick something up from the floor of Luke's office.

He glanced at the scalloped, gilt-edged card she was holding. Damn, he hadn't noticed he'd missed his aim.

'Nothing,' he said. 'It was supposed to go in the bin.'

'But…' Anna was reading the fancy calligraphy and then she looked up with a stunned expression on her face. 'Luke…this is an invitation to a medal ceremony, isn't it? Returning Heroes. With a ball to honour the recipients of the medals.'

'I'm not going. I hate parties.' Luke swivelled his desk chair so that he could drop a file into the cabinet behind him. 'Was there something you wanted to talk to me about?'

'Yes.'

Another file tab caught Luke's eye and he pulled it out. It took several seconds to register the silence. Anna wasn't going to talk to him until she was confident he was listening.

Fine. He swung the chair back around. 'What do you want to talk about?'

She was still holding the card and looked down at it again. 'This.'

'That's not why you came in here. You didn't know it existed.' He could feel his eyes narrowing as he sighed. 'What was the real reason you came in?'

'This isn't even an invitation. It says you're "required to attend". That sounds pretty official. Will you get into trouble if you don't go?'

Luke gave a huff of laughter. 'What can they do? Kick me out of the army? Give my medal to someone else? That's fine by me. I don't want the damn medal.'

'Why not?' Anna sank into the other chair in

his office but her gaze was unwavering. Fixed on Luke. She wasn't going to let this one go.

He felt trapped. Angry. The way he had ever since he'd woken from that nightmare to find Anna in his bed. This was becoming a problem. OK, the sex was great. She was great. He loved seeing her like this, at work, in her neat clothes and with her hair all scraped back. Being completely professional in their interactions while all the time they both knew what it would be like after, away from work.

When the clothes came off and the communication came through touch and not words. When they could both escape to a place that promised only pleasure.

But maybe it had run its course. It wasn't going to work. Not long term.

She was already too close. Had seen too much. She didn't represent a rope that he could use to help him into his future any more. She was starting to resemble a roadway. With traffic in both directions. He didn't want to go back. He couldn't. Because if he did, he would be taking Anna with him and she would see who he really was and then she would be the one to go.

And that might finally destroy him.

Anna could see the play of emotion on Luke's face. The annoyance that she was pushing when he'd made it clear he wasn't interested in either going to this ceremony or talking about it. She knew perfectly well she was stepping over a boundary here. She could almost see him weighing up whether she was worth the trouble.

Would he tell her to get out? Push so hard she had no choice but to leave? He'd been holding her at a distance ever since that nightmare. They hadn't been to bed together for three days now. They hadn't even spent that much time together at work. He was avoiding her because he didn't want to talk about the nightmare. Probably didn't want to admit how often he had them. Or that they happened at all, like the flashbacks. Talking about this medal ceremony and what it had to remind him of might tip them over the edge and it would all be over, but it was a risk Anna had no choice but to take.

Maybe Luke needed a push himself to recognize that he had PTSD. He had to be willing to confront his past. She was quite prepared to help him and be with him through any rough patches but only if it was part of a healing process. Otherwise she would just be locking herself into a miserable cycle of watching the man she loved suffer. Getting pushed away and hurt herself and then crawling back for more of the same.

She wasn't going to do it. If she did, she would only be allowing Luke to stay locked in that dark space permanently and he was worth more than that.

'Why not, Luke?' she asked again. 'Why don't you want to get the recognition you deserve? It's your name that's right at the top of that list.

Does your family know about this? Will they be there, hoping to be part of the honour?'

'I don't want the damned medal.' The words burst out in an angry rush as Luke leaned forward on his desk, both hands clenched into fists. 'I haven't told my family because I don't want to celebrate what happened. Or to glorify war. To pretty it up for the media with everyone in nice, clean uniforms and rows of shiny badges. Dancing, for God's sake! That's about as meaningless as everything else in civilian life.' He lowered his voice and it became rough. Totally compelling. 'War is about blood and guts and people. People who can be terrified they're not going to get back to the ones they love. Who can die, in agony, a thousand miles away from the people who love them.'

He tipped his head back, closing his eyes. 'Yes, I survived. But what about all the others?'

Slowly, he brought his gaze back to Anna's. His eyes were dark. So shadowed they were blank of emotion. Like the rest of his face. 'I don't want a prize for being one of the lucky ones.'

Anna swallowed. Hard. She was part of his civilian life. Meaningless.

The silence stretched on. Tense and horrible. She had to say something. To try and defuse this awful distance escalating between them.

'Yes, war is about people,' she said finally. 'That's how they generally start, isn't it? You have a group of people, including innocent children, who lose their lives or have their rights as human beings threatened or taken away. Most people have to try and close their minds to the atrocities that go on because it doesn't affect their lives and they can't do anything about it, anyway.' She drew in a breath, the words coming more easily now. 'But some people are brave enough to put their hands up and say, I'll help. I'll go into horrible places and endure terrible things. Not because I might end up getting a medal for it but because it might—eventually—help to make the world a better place.'

Was he listening? Anna couldn't tell. She was talking hard and fast now, barely forming the thoughts before the words tumbled from her mouth. Desperately trying to let Luke know, somehow, that it was all right to have this as part of his past. That she accepted it. And if she talked enough, maybe by some miracle she could say something that would get through to him. Stop him from shutting her out and pushing her out of his life.

'If enough people didn't avoid even thinking about wars, maybe something could change without people having to die,' she continued. 'And maybe the publicity that comes from something like this is what makes them take notice. It's the heroes that people can't help taking notice of. That they listen to.'

Luke was staring at her now but his face was still devoid of emotion.

'Maybe the people who take the most notice are the ones who've lost someone they love. Because they have to try and make sense of it all.'

Which was exactly what Luke needed to do himself, wasn't it?

'Or maybe it's the people who will feel lucky for the rest of their lives because someone they love has come home. Thanks to one of those heroes. I'll bet the families of all the soldiers you saved would love to give you a medal, Luke, but they don't have to, do they? The army is going to do it for them.'

Still no reaction. Anna felt a flicker of anger. 'How do you think they'll feel if you can't be bothered to show up?'

That did it. Luke's face finally moved but it was only to turn away from her. 'Are you finished?'

'No.' Anna's mouth had gone dry. This was it. She had failed. He wasn't going to let her into this part of his life. Her breath came out in a ragged sigh. She closed her eyes in defeat. 'The party wouldn't be so bad,' she said dryly. 'At least nobody would be wearing reindeer horns.'

Opening her eyes, she found Luke had turned

back to face her. For a heartbeat her flippant comment hung in the air and then she saw a change in Luke's eyes. A lightening of those shadows. A vaguely incredulous expression that took her back to…

Oh, help. Back to that day when Luke had come to her cottage and discovered Anna instead of his colleague, Dr Bartlett. When she'd made that stupid joke about unlikely dogs using a staircase to become mates. So she was no good at cracking jokes? Did he have to look at her as though he was seeing someone he didn't even recognise?

Someone stupid, maybe, who said meaningless things that made him wonder why on earth he'd ever been attracted to her?

But Luke's lips were moving now.

Good grief! He was smiling. Virtually grinning.

'OK,' he said. 'I'll go. On one condition.'

'What's that?' The relief that he wasn't shouting at her or physically throwing her out of his office was enormous. It was making her feel light-headed. Ridiculously happy.

Hopeful, even.

'That you come with me.'

Anna's head cleared astonishingly quickly. An image of a military ball sprang into her head. Men in dress uniform. Luke in dress uniform. He would look impossibly gorgeous. And she would have to be dressed up and feminine. No way would she be on ground where she could feel like an equal. But they weren't equal, were they? Even here. Not on emotional grounds, anyway.

She would be so proud of him if she went. She would be getting herself in ever deeper.

But wasn't that what she wanted? Needed? Or was it that she knew she should fight it but just couldn't help herself?

Anna shook her head, trying to clear the confused jumble of her thoughts. Luke misinterpreted the gesture as reluctance.

'You think I should go,' he said. 'And you're probably correct.'

Another memory was niggling at Anna now. She'd persuaded Luke to attend the staff Christmas function by telling him that heads of departments would be expected to attend. Look what had happened there. How much more likely would a flashback be when he was surrounded by army uniforms and by people wanting to talk about why he was being honoured as a hero?

'I won't go unless you come with me,' Luke said quietly. 'Please, Anna. I...need you.'

Three little words. Possibly the only three she'd ever hear from Luke but maybe they were enough.

'All right,' she said with a catch in her voice. 'I'll come with you.'

Why had he been so determined not to attend this event?

So bad-tempered about having to put on his

dress uniform 'Blues' and act like a soldier? Gritting his teeth as he'd accepted all the congratulations that came with the medal now pinned to his tunic.

Hating it all so much he'd barely spoken to Anna, even though he could see how much effort she'd put into this on his behalf. Buying a new dress and having her hair done in some fancy way. Putting up with his foul mood for the whole of their drive to London. All those long stretches when the only sound in the vehicle had been the windscreen wipers trying to cope with the sleet of the January evening.

He'd only asked her to dance because it was the last duty he had to perform tonight. The recipients of the medals and their partners had been invited to take the floor first and people were watching. Clapping.

One dance and then he could escape. Drive back to St Piran, apologise to Anna and then forget the whole excruciating business.

The lighting was softened as the orchestra

began playing a waltz. Chandeliers still sparkled overhead and the reflection of the crowd present could be seen in the glass of the floor-to-ceiling windows that filled one wall and afforded a spectacular view of London beyond. Diamonds glistened on women and the buttons on dress uniforms gleamed on the men.

Holding out his hand to Anna, Luke had the sudden, awful thought that he hadn't bothered to find out if Anna knew how to dance something formal. He'd had lessons as a teenager, along with all his brothers, and the skill was automatic. Not that he'd had either the opportunity or the desire to use it for a very long time. But Anna took his hand and came into his arms willingly. The dark, emerald fabric of her long dress shimmered in this lighting and he gathered her into a formal dance hold. Stiffly at first, until the steps came more easily. It was only then that he noticed how light Anna was on her feet and how well she was able to follow his lead.

More couples came onto the dance floor but Luke didn't even notice. In his relief that he wasn't embarrassing Anna and making her evening even worse than he had already by assuming a skill she might not have, he relaxed a notch. Another notch or two got added when he remembered that the evening was almost over. He was going to get through it. And that was when he finally looked down and really noticed the woman in his arms.

Her hair had been scooped up in some clever fashion to make coils that sat sleekly against the back of her head. Little bits had been pulled free, however, so that tiny soft spirals framed her face and drew attention to the lovely length of her neck. The style was formal and precise—like Anna was at work—but it was those free tendrils that Luke really liked. They reminded him of the way Anna was when she wasn't at work. Softer. Surprising.

Pure woman.

The fabric of her dress was silky under his

hands. Almost as delicious as he knew her bare skin to be. The colour was sheer brilliance. How had it taken him this long to notice how it was a shade or two darker than her eyes and made them so...luminous.

So extraordinarily beautiful.

Mesmerising.

The music altered tempo as the orchestra started something less classical. Something moody and sweet. It was the perfect opportunity to make an exit from the dance floor but Luke had lost any desire to do so. Instead, he drew Anna closer. He wasn't following any routine steps now, just moving to the music that surrounded them. Holding an amazingly beautiful woman who followed every move he made so easily it was like holding an extension to his own body.

She looked and felt so lovely. She even smelled so wonderful that Luke bent his head to get closer. Was that perfume coming from her hair or her skin? Or was it just Anna? It was hypnotising. A new space. An escape that was better than sleep. Better than sex, even, because he could keep this up for ever.

He certainly wasn't going to be the one to suggest stopping any time soon.

Anna had been very close to tears by the time Luke asked her to dance.

Wishing she'd never agreed to accompany him. A million miles away from this would have been too close. She'd tried so hard to look the part and he'd been so closed off and angry from the moment he'd arrived at her door to collect her.

The drive had been awful. Full of silences during which she had nothing to think about except the distance between them. That she was no closer to imagining a way out of this for Luke that could offer the promise of a happy future for him.

For them both.

Watching him during the ceremonial part

of the evening had been even more grim. He looked just as gorgeous as she'd expected in the crisp, dark blue uniform with its braid and insignia, but she'd been able to see how much he'd been hating it. Tension so great it seemed like he could simply snap at any moment. Luke hadn't wanted to be a part of any of this. He hadn't wanted any of it to be a part of his past.

Could no one else see what she could see? That the event that had led to him being here tonight was what had scarred him so deeply. That he was determined to escape the memories and he couldn't see that the only way to stop them haunting him to the point of ruining his life was to turn round and confront them.

The tension had been contagious. All Anna had wanted was for the evening to end. To get through that long drive home somehow and then…what?

Admit defeat and see what she could do about putting her life back together the way it had been before Luke had come back to St Piran?

It had been the thought of trying to move on without him that had been what nearly brought her to tears in public. But then Luke had held out his hand when the medal recipients had been invited to take the dance floor first. It had been the first time he'd touched her in what felt like a very, very long time, and as soon as Anna had felt that contact she'd known exactly where she really wanted to be.

Not a million miles away at all.

Right here.

In Luke's arms.

He could dance. When the initial awkwardness wore off, Anna was astonished to find he could actually dance beautifully. The music was soothing and the rhythm of the waltz easy to follow even from long-ago lessons. Glancing up, she found Luke's face still grim and turned away. He was going through the motions here, but in reality he was hunting for an escape route.

Dropping her gaze, Anna stared at the medal pinned to his tunic, awarded for an act of outstanding bravery during active operations against an enemy. It was a beautiful silver cross mounted on a wreath of laurel leaves with a crown in its centre. The ribbon had narrow stripes of dark blue on each edge and a central stripe of crimson. What would he do with it when he got home? Shut it away in its box and hide it along with the memories of why it had been bestowed?

Looking up again, Anna was startled to find Luke's gaze on her face. An intense gaze but one she was getting used to. As though he was seeing her properly for the first time. Looking... amazed.

The waltz ended and Anna knew this would be when Luke suggested they sit down or go to supper perhaps. Or just go home.

Instead, he drew her closer and she could feel some of that terrible tension leaving his body. They were so close. She could feel the length of his body against hers. Leading her. So powerful and yet it felt gentle, probably because she was so willing to follow.

And then she felt his cheek against her hair and Anna closed her eyes, sinking into the delicious knowledge that Luke wasn't just dancing now.

He was dancing with her.

Another medley of tunes began. And then another, but Luke made no move to take her away from the dance floor and Anna certainly wasn't going to be the one to break this connection.

She wanted it to last for ever.

The start of the fireworks display startled all the guests. The wall of windows provided a great view of the city lights on the other side of the Thames but nobody had noticed the grassy bank-side area until the impressive display got under way.

It began with a sound like a cannon firing. A huge silver rocket shot up into the blackness of the sky and then exploded into a shower of tiny silver spheres that drifted down slowly.

Not that Anna was watching them. At the first sound Luke had stiffened so abruptly that she had tripped on his foot. Then he moved again, so sharply Anna could swear she felt him snap. He dropped his arms from her body and turned swiftly, weaving between couples who had also stopped dancing to see what was happening. They began to move towards the windows.

Anna moved in the opposite direction. Following Luke. All the way out of the ball-room. Through the area where a buffet supper was being served. Through the vast foyer where staff were now stacking all the chairs that had been used for the initial ceremony. Down a wide flight of steps. She could feel the sting of sleet on her skin. Gathering up the folds of her dress, she raced after Luke. Around the corner of the building. As far away as he could get from where the fireworks were happening.

And there he stopped. When Anna came

around the corner she saw him, his head on his arm, leaning against the stone wall. She could hear him gasping for breath in the same way he had when he'd been having that nightmare.

'Luke!'

'Go, Anna.' The plea was hoarse. 'Get out. While you can.'

She came up to be right beside him. 'I'm not going anywhere. Talk to me.'

'I can't.'

At least part of him was there and aware of her. He'd been like that in the canteen too, hadn't he? Having a flashback he couldn't control but still aware of things around him, like bumping into someone and spilling their drink. Maybe, if she tried hard enough, she could get through to him.

'Why not?' she begged. 'Why can't you talk to me, Luke?'

'My problem. If I told you, it would become your problem.' The words were staccato. Agonised. 'I won't do that to you.'

'It's already my problem.'

'No. You can go. I want you to go.'

'I can't do that, Luke.'

'Why the hell not?' His head turned and the expression on his face broke her heart.

'Because…because I love you, that's why.'

Luke buried his head again and he groaned. It was a sound of such distress but was it due to her confession or because of whatever still had him in its grip?

Fireworks were still going off, muted a little by the vast building between them but still loud. Possibly loud enough that he hadn't heard what she'd just said. Or maybe he had chosen not to hear it because he already had too much to deal with.

'It's the noise, isn't it?' She had to touch Luke. To get closer. 'Where are you, Luke? What do you see?'

A moment's silence and then Luke spoke in a low, desperate voice she barely recognised.

'We're under fire. We're on our way to a village. There's children hurt by a landmine but we don't get there.' The words were rushing out so fast it was hard to hear them clearly. 'It's an ambush. Another mine. And artillery. The truck's tipped over. Everybody's hurt. I…I felt my leg snap.'

He dragged in a breath. 'We need to get out. Danny's unconscious. His airway's blocked. There's a chopper coming. I can smell the smoke and the blood. The guys are screaming. I'm trapped. I'm trying to get them out and I can't move. I can't breathe…'

Anna was gripping his arm. 'Yes, you can, Luke. You did get them out. All of them. That's why you got the medal tonight. You saved everybody in that truck. You saved their lives.'

'But I didn't…' Luke groaned again. Or was it a sob? 'Not the life I wanted to save.' Yes, it was definitely a sob now. Torn from somewhere deep inside. 'I couldn't save Crash, Anna. I… wanted to…so much…and I…couldn't…'

Racking sobs took hold of Luke's body now. All Anna could do was to hold him as hard as she could and be there. Saying nothing. Letting him hold her so tightly it was impossible to take a deep breath and letting him rock her as he rocked himself.

And eventually, as she became aware of how damp and cold they were both going to be, Luke quietened.

'Let's go home,' she said.

Luke waited outside while she collected their coats and the car keys.

'I can drive if you'd like.'

'No. I'm all right.' Luke's voice was sombre. 'Better if I'm doing something. I'm sorry about that.'

'I'm not,' Anna said, but Luke didn't hear her. He was striding ahead to where the car was parked.

Sleet was still falling and got thicker as they left the outskirts of London but the road was still clear enough. Anna listened to the windscreen wipers. They sounded different now. Maybe because the atmosphere inside the car wasn't as charged as it had been coming in the opposite direction. The tension was gone. Luke seemed tired but calm.

'Who was Crash?' Anna asked softly. 'A friend?'

'My brother. His real name was Matthew. Mattie.'

'Oh...'

Anna was searching her memory. She'd known that name had come from something special. A kid who'd grown too fast, he'd said, and looked a bit goofy with big feet. So clumsy he'd earned the nickname of Crash. He grown into...what had Luke said? Oh, yes. The strongest, bravest guy he knew.

And then he'd given her that first smile. The one that had melted her heart.

'He was younger than you?' The question was tentative. It seemed too good to believe that Luke was finally talking to her.

Letting her in.

'Yeah.' Luke's gaze was fixed on the road ahead. He was driving a little below the speed limit. Taking it carefully.

Anna felt safe with him but did he feel the same way?

'There's an older brother, too,' Luke said after a moment. 'The Davenport boys, we were called. A collective troop. A mini-platoon. Nobody questioned that we would do anything but take after our dad and join the army.'

'It must have been hard for you, then.'

'Yeah.' The word was heartfelt. 'I felt guilty. Especially after Crash joined up. I'd always tried to look out for him, you know? In the end, though, he was looking out for me. He was the only one who understood why I wanted to be a civilian. A doctor.'

Anna couldn't ask the obvious question but it was hanging there and Luke could sense it.

'He got killed in action in Iraq,' he said very softly. 'And it just broke me up. I owed him so much. I missed him so badly. In the end, the answer seemed easy. I joined up to honour his memory. To do what I should have done all along. I thought it would make me feel less guilty. That it would somehow help fill the horrible, empty, useless feeling I had.'

A long silence this time and then Luke sighed. 'All I really achieved was to screw up the rest of my life. I'm not fit to do my job any more. I'm not a viable proposition to be in any kind of a meaningful relationship. I meant what I said, Anna. You should get out. Relatively unscathed. While you still can.'

'And I meant what I said,' Anna whispered. She wasn't going to tell him again that she loved him. It was enough to know she had said it aloud and it was true. Instinct told her he wasn't ready to hear those particular words but she could remind him of something else she'd said. 'I'm not going anywhere. We all need courage to face the future,' she added carefully. 'It's not a sign of weakness if you have to ask for help sometimes.'

Maybe she could remind him of something he'd said, too. 'You're the strongest, bravest man I know,' she said, deliberately using the words he'd used to describe his brother. 'You'll make it.'

This wasn't the time to talk about finding the help Luke needed or how to find it. They'd made enough of a breakthrough tonight. All Anna wanted now was to get home and go to bed. With Luke.

And sleep. She was so tired. The windscreen wipers flicked in a steady rhythm. Swirls of tiny white flakes zoomed towards them in a hypnotic pattern. Anna could feel her eyes drifting closed.

She was sound asleep, Luke noticed, as they finally left the main roads behind. The snow began falling more thickly and he slowed their pace. He didn't like the deteriorating conditions but he could take his time getting them home. Funny, but he felt like he had all the time he needed now. For anything. He couldn't remember when he'd last felt this…peaceful? Maybe he never had.

He stole another glance at Anna. He would get her home safely. He knew the road and he could cope with the weather.

What he couldn't control was the other traffic on the road that night. Especially when he had no warning of what was coming around the corner. The driver of the big truck probably didn't realise how far his wheels were over the centre line of the coastal road because the snow was starting to settle in patches and the road markings were fading.

The jolt of leaving the smooth road surface and then hitting a fence post woke Anna and all Luke could hear as he fought desperately to prevent the car tipping into a roll was her scream of fear.

CHAPTER TEN

ANNA'S scream was cut off abruptly with the first impact of the rolling vehicle but the sound of metal shearing and scraping on rock was another kind of scream. Airbags deployed with a blast and shockwave that was indistinguishable from gunfire.

Luke was inside his nightmare but he knew he was awake and that made it so much worse. So confusing. His mind was being rocked and jolted as viciously as his body. One moment hanging in the straps of his safety belt, the next jarring on solid ground. A maelstrom of fear and desperation. The past, the present and things that had never been real, and never would be, existing only in his imagination.

He was in an army vehicle again but not the one in which he'd met the end of his time at war.

In one that he'd never actually seen or touched. Just imagined. The one his brother, Matthew, had been driving. And each time they hit solid ground, they were hitting the mine that had destroyed the person he loved most in the world. Once, twice...three hits and he was still alive and awake.

This time, he had to save him.

Or he would die himself.

The violent churning of the landscape, vehicle and people probably lasted no more than thirty seconds but it felt like for ever. And then there was silence. A broken headlamp flickered for a second or two and then died.

It was pitch black and utterly silent.

Luke had been convinced that the worst sound he could ever hear were the screams of frightened and dying men, any one of whom could be his brother. Even the terrified sound Anna had made had become the last breath Crash had expelled.

In that instant, however, he knew the real truth.

That silence was far worse.

Crash.

Blindly, Luke reached out. His fingers caught in the limp, metallic folds of airbags that had erupted from the steering-wheel, the centre console and the dashboard.

'Can you hear me?'

A tiny sound in the silence as he strained to listen. An indrawn breath. Tentative and ragged.

'Y-yes.'

It wasn't Crash. It was Anna.

Of course it was. He'd known that all along. Hadn't he?

And she was alive, thank God. 'Are you hurt?'

'I...I'm not sure...'

He had to move. To find a source of light and then check Anna out. He had to get her out of this and make sure she would be all right. Any other course of action or result was unthinkable.

But his head swam when he tried to move.

Impossible to tell which way was supposed to be up. Had the car ended up on its roof instead of its wheels? Was it really Anna?

Luke found the catch of his safety belt and released it. His body didn't start falling so he wasn't upside down. His head started to clear.

'Take a deep breath,' he told Anna. 'As deep as you can.'

He listened to her comply with his request.

'Is it difficult? Does anything hurt?'

'N-no…'

'Can you move your arms? God, it's so dark. I can't see anything. Does your neck hurt? Don't move your head if it does.'

He could hear Anna shift position. Could see a change of shape in the darkness.

'I…I can move.'

So could Luke. He turned and began to lean sideways so that his hands could reach Anna's huddled figure on the far side of the vehicle. She was lower than he was. The car was on some kind of slope.

And then he froze.

It wasn't his head swimming this time. It was the car that was moving.

Rocking gently.

There was a scratching, scraping sound coming from somewhere beneath them. Metal on rock. And Luke became aware of another sound. He hadn't noticed it before because it could have been the rush of his own blood pulsing in his head.

Somewhere, far below, waves were rolling onto rocks.

They had been on a coastal road that often came close to clifftop. There had been a fence of some kind. A farmer's field or a barrier that was there to prevent anyone getting too close to a dangerous place? Like one that had a sheer drop to rocks that would not be survivable?

Perhaps it was just as well it was too dark to see anything outside.

Cold, damp air was coming in with the sounds of the night. Luke's door seemed to be missing or crumpled to leave an open space. Survival instinct was trying to kick in. The upward ground was on his side and he had an escape route. Even if the car was teetering on the top of a cliff, he could make a dive for it and roll free.

But that would change the weight distribution dramatically and that might be all that was needed to tip the vehicle and send it plunging over the edge.

With Anna still inside.

He would rather die himself.

The car was still rocking. Scraping.

'Luke?' Anna's whisper was terrified. 'What's…happening?'

'Don't move,' he said softly. 'Give me a sec. I need to think.'

Fear was clawing at him now. A dense cloud that contained a kaleidoscope of images and emotions that paralysed Luke for a moment. Sucking him into the place he couldn't allow himself to go.

No.

He couldn't smell blood. Or smoke. Or dust. Nobody was screaming.

They were in a car, not an armoured vehicle. This was Anna. Not Crash.

So why was it just as important that she was going to be all right? Crash was the person he had loved with all his heart. The one he would have given his own life to save.

It had taken a split second for Luke to understand the truth that silence could be more dreadful than any scream.

The truth he now learned arrived with similar, blinding clarity.

He had only been confused about the person he needed to save because of an emotion he hadn't allowed himself to entertain.

He loved Anna.

A different kind of love than he'd had for Crash but it was just as powerful. More so, even. He'd been kidding himself thinking of her as his rope. Or anchor. Or any other kind of tool to help him find his own future.

She was that future.

From that first moment when he'd found himself under her resentful glare she had entered his consciousness. His mind and—slipping somehow under a defensive radar—his heart.

'Luke...' Anna was crying. 'Talk to me. Are you hurt?'

'I'm fine.' He moved his hand carefully, just far enough to grip hers. 'As long as you are.'

'What happened?'

'We've had an accident. There was a truck. It came around a corner on the wrong side of the road. I had to swerve and... Oh, God, I'm sorry, Anna.'

The grip on his hand tightened. 'That doesn't matter. We just need to get out.'

'We have to be careful. I'm not sure how stable the car is and I don't want it to move.'

'I'm scared.'

'I know. I am too but we'll get through this, Anna. Together.'

'Are you sure you're all right? It's not… I mean… You know…like a flashback thing?'

Oh, yes. The flashbacks he'd never admitted to. He couldn't admit to loving Anna either, could he? What did he have to offer her? He was broken.

'I want to get out. I want to get home.'

'I know. We will. I'll get you out, Anna. I'll take care of you.'

There was a light outside now. Coming closer. A powerful torch that filled the interior of this battered car in a sweeping motion. For a heart-beat Luke could see Anna's face clearly. The way she was looking at him.

She wasn't going anywhere, she'd said—way back before the accident had happened. She'd said she loved him.

He could see that love in her eyes. He could fall into it. Return it? How much courage would that take? What if he failed her, as he had failed his brother? If he lost her…

'Anna…I—'

The light got brighter. Steadier. A man's voice called out. 'Whatever you do in there, don't move. I've got a chain in the truck and I'm going to get it onto the back of your car. Help's on the way.'

Luke didn't want to move. Neither, it seemed, did Anna. The grip on his hand was tight enough to impair circulation.

'Don't let go of me,' she begged. 'Please. Not yet.'

'I won't,' he vowed. I can't, he added silently, because I love you.

The nearest hospital was St Piran's.

Ben Carter was astonished to find Anna and Luke turning up in the emergency department, dressed up to the nines, in the early hours of the morning but he was more amazed to be able to give them a medical all-clear not long afterwards.

'You're both incredibly lucky. A few bumps

and bruises but nothing that a good sleep won't help.'

Anna caught Luke's wry glance. As if a good sleep was remotely likely for him even when he hadn't been through such a traumatic few hours. It was a private exchange. Ben didn't see it because he was shaking his head.

'I can't imagine what it must have felt like, seeing your car going over that cliff when the chain broke. The rescue guys are going to be talking about their good timing for years to come.'

'So will we,' Anna said. She smiled at Luke. 'Let's go and see if that taxi's here yet.'

They went to Luke's house because it was closer and Anna was still worried about the effects the accident might have had on Luke that no X-ray or examination would have picked up.

To have had this happen today, of all days, when he had been starting to open up to her about the past that haunted him so badly. No wonder he was so quiet now. And why he made no move to make love to her when they went straight to bed. They were both utterly exhausted but Anna was determined to stay awake. To be ready to hold Luke when he had the nightmare she was sure would come.

At some point, however, she fell asleep because it was impossible not to. When she awoke to find winter sunlight warming the room, she gasped in horror. Had she slept through Luke waking? Going to outrun his demons on the beach or dispel them with an arctic swim? He never missed his dawn swim.

But he was still there. Beside her. One arm draped over her body. Her gasp must have woken him because his eyes were open.

'You OK?'

Anna nodded. 'I'm sorry...'

'What for?'

'I must have slept through you getting up. I didn't mean to. I wanted...'

Luke was staring at her with an odd expression.

'What?' she breathed. 'What's wrong?'

'I didn't get up,' he said slowly. 'I didn't even wake up.'

'You slept through the whole night?'

'What was left of it, anyway.' He blinked at her, disbelief still etched on his features. 'That's hours. Hours and hours and hours.'

Anna's lips trembled as they stretched into a smile. 'How do you feel?'

'Different…' Luke's gaze dropped to Anna's lips and then dropped further. 'Hungry.'

'You want breakfast?'

'No.' He looked up again and smiled. 'I want… you.'

Anna snuggled closer, raising her face to meet Luke's kiss. 'I want you, too.'

'You're not too sore or anything?'

'A bit stiff and achy. Nothing that a walk on the beach in some sunshine won't cure.'

'Soon.' Luke's lips brushed hers gently and then came back as he sighed. 'Or maybe not that soon.'

His mouth claimed hers this time and Anna surrendered willingly. The walk could wait.

The last day of January found them walking on the beach.

A dawn walk that had become a firm habit now. Crash was with them, loping around on his big, puppy feet with a stick of driftwood clamped between his teeth.

'You're supposed to bring it back,' Luke called.

'He wants you to chase him.'

'That won't help his retrieving training.'

'No.' Besides, Anna didn't want to let go of Luke's hand. She loved this time of day with him. In the soft light and breathing the fresh, cold air. Walking so close they often leaned on each other as well as holding hands. And sometimes, as they did right now, they would stop and watch the waves rolling in for a minute or two.

'You haven't been for a swim since the accident.'

'No. I don't need to any more.'

Anna gave Luke a questioning glance but he was still staring at the waves.

'When I came back from Iraq,' he said a moment later, 'it seemed like I had no connection here any more. Or anywhere. Part of me was still over there. Caught up in the frenetic battle to save lives. To stay alive. Civilian life seemed empty. Meaningless.'

Still Anna said nothing. She couldn't. She remembered Luke saying something about that and she hadn't forgotten thinking that she had been included in the things that had no meaning. She knew that wasn't true. Maybe Luke hadn't told her as such but he was showing her. Every day. In so many ways.

'It made me numb, swimming in a freezing sea and getting tossed around by the surf,' Luke continued quietly. 'And it helped…then. I don't need to be numb now. I don't want to be, even for a moment.' He turned his head and looked down at Anna.

'Because even if it was just for the length of time it took to have that swim, it would be too long to feel numb. I don't want to give up a second of the most amazing feeling I could ever have.'

Anna's breath caught. She knew the answer but had to ask the question. To hear the words spoken aloud. 'What is it…that feeling?'

'My love for you.'

His kiss tasted of the sea and it was slow and exquisitely tender. Anna stood on tiptoe and wrapped her arms around his neck. It took the impatient bark of a large puppy to bring them back to the present moment. Luke laughed, stooped to pick up the stick that had been placed right beside his feet and threw it again. Then he took Anna's hand in his and they began walking again, a triumphant Crash making wide circles around them with the stick back in his jaws.

'I love you, Anna,' Luke said. 'You are the

reason I want to get up in the mornings and the reason I can't wait to get to bed at night. I hope I never have to have a night or day without you to share it with but…' He took a deep breath and let it out in a sigh. 'I'm not going to ask you to marry me. I can't.'

Anna's feet stopped without any such instruction from her brain. Her hand tugged at Luke's a heartbeat later and he had to stop, too. She stared at him. The shadows in his eyes had begun to lift in the last week or so but the sadness she could still see in his face was heartbreaking.

'I can't offer you anything,' Luke said. 'I've lost my job.'

Anna gave her head a slow shake. 'You didn't lose it. You had the courage to go and talk to Mr White about everything and he had the good sense to persuade you to go onto the board of directors for St Piran's. You're going to be a brilliant administrator, Luke, and it's not as if you're not going to be part of the department for teaching—'

'Your department now,' Luke interrupted.

Anna looked away. It was so weird to think she had wanted to hang onto that position so badly that she would have preferred Luke to have never come back to St Piran's.

'I have PTSD,' Luke said into the silence. 'An official diagnosis from a qualified shrink.'

'An eminent psychiatrist who specialises in cognitive-behavioural therapy,' Anna corrected with a smile. 'Someone who thinks you're making amazing progress already.'

She watched a wave roll in. And then another. And then she turned to face Luke again.

'All you ever need to offer me is your love, Luke.'

He was watching her face with that intent gaze of his. Listening carefully. Waiting to hear what she would say next.

'And I don't want you to ask me to marry you,' she said.

She saw him swallow hard. Saw a flicker of doubt—fear, almost—in his eyes.

Anna smiled. 'Because I'm going to ask you.'

She took a deep breath. This shouldn't be so hard, should it? She'd been competing in a man's world for long enough to be able to tackle anything.

'I love you, Luke Davenport. With all my heart. I don't want to have a single night or day without you in it either. Will you marry me?'

He was still staring at her. One of those looks—as if he was seeing her for the very first time.

'Um… Please?' she added.

His arms came around her with such speed that Anna squeaked as she felt herself grabbed and lifted. She was being whirled round and round and the world was spinning.

'Yes,' Luke said. 'Yes.'

He stopped whirling her but was still holding her well off the ground, his hands around her waist. Her hands were on his shoulders as he slowly lowered her enough for their lips to touch.

A new wave came in, leading the incoming tide further up the beach, and it reached far enough to swirl around Luke's ankles and splash Anna's legs with pure ice.

Luke dropped one arm to catch Anna behind her knees. He scooped her into his arms and carried her through the still foaming wave to dry sand but he didn't put her down. Crash followed as they left the beach to go home and get ready for their new day. And still Luke hadn't put Anna down.

And that was just fine by her.

She was exactly where she wanted to be. Moving into her future, cradled in the arms of the man she would always love.

* * * * *